STEAMPUNK

MACHINATIONS

AN ESSENTIAL RULES EXPANSION OF THE
IMMORTAL EMPIRES™
ROLE-PLAYING GAME FOR MATURE PLAYERS

Acknowledgements

Special thanks goes to the following people who helped in the development, test playing, and history of the game:

Writers & Developers & Contributors

B. Joshua (Writer/Developer/Maps)

J. Becht (Ideas Contributor (Some Vocations/Cyber Age Hostilities Beta thoughts))

J. Carney (Ideas Contributor (Günther))

T. Helvey (Ideas Contributor/The Nitty Gritty/Modern Armor & Weaponry)

Illustrations

Cover Design: Pixel Perfect Publishing (Melinda Burt)

Andrey Kiselev (52, 53, 54, 61, 62, 63, 69, 70a, 71b), Fernando Cortes (56), Michael Rosskothen (30)

zabelin (60), 3355m (48a), Scott Griessel (57), Yuri Iluhin (58), NeiroN (64), Burmakin Andrey (39, 59, 68, 70b, 71a, 71c)

ateliersommerland (Cover image: airship), katalinks (55), Joerg Michael Gehrke (20), shamain (26)

Alexander Gorlov (50a), lightfieldstudios (50b), bfm2218 (48b), Fernando Gregory Milan (69), Luis Louro (49)

Anna Ivanova (38), Victor Zastolskiy (41), Pavel Zhovba (Cover image: submersible)

Steampunk Machinations: an Essential Rules Expansion of the Immortal Empires Role-Playing Game for Mature Players

Copyright © 2020 JITT HOLDINGS, Inc.

86p. 8.5"x11" Full Color Paperback.

ISBN-13: 978-0-578-64517-9

BISAC: Fiction/Fantasy/General // Games & Activities/Role Playing & Fantasy

Table of Contents

Players

Storytellers

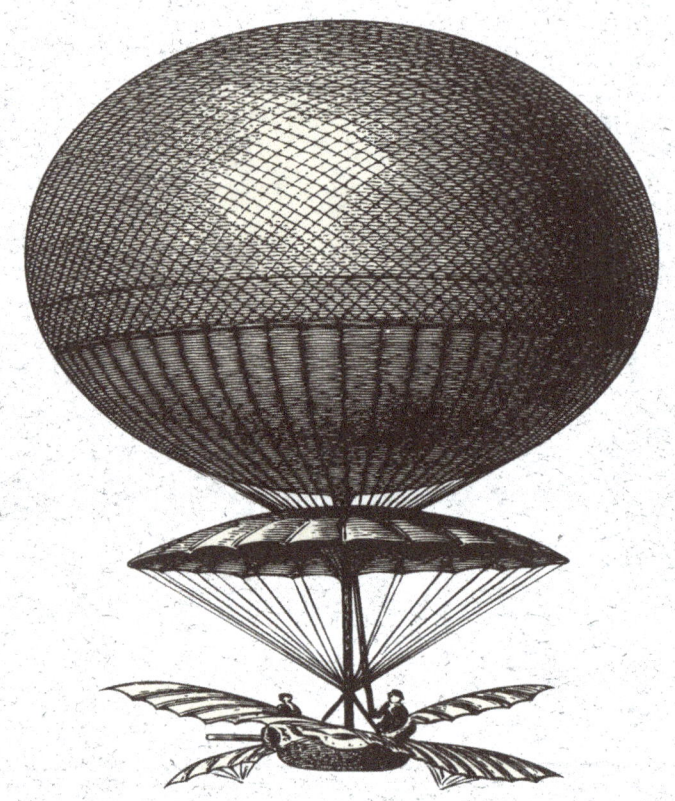

STEAMPUNK IS AN ECLECTIC WORLD
OF COGS AND RIVETS. IT IS AIRSHIPS,
GOGGLES AND STEAM. IT IS ROMANCE.
IT IS TRAVELING ON CLOUDS AND DIVING
BENEATH RUGGED WAVES.

IT IS ADVENTURE.

—AETHER EMPORIUM—

WHY STEAMPUNK

PART ONE

PREAMBLE...

Thank you for purchasing IMMORTAL EMPIRES™ Steampunk Machinations expansion. It is a continuation of the Official Storyline and as such uses the same game system. The Steampunk expansion is fully compatible with the Storyteller's Codex, The Adventurer's Rulebook, and the Cyber Age Hostilities rules expansion.

In order to run an Immortal Empires Steampunk game, you'll need the following:

— Adventurer's Guidebook
— Storyteller's Codex
— Cyber Age Hostilities rules expansion (Optional)
— Phase Combat Chart
— 15 Ten-sided dice
(10 White, 3 Blue, 2 Gold)
— 1 Red ten-sided Penalty Die
— Hex Map and Plastic Overlay
— One Master Character Record**
(for copying)

We've divided this book into two parts. The first part is for all eyes: Players and Storytellers alike. The second part is for the Storyteller's eyes alone. Of course, it's an honor code, but you may ruin your own fun if you aren't the Storyteller and look anyway!

** The Character Record you use can be either the Legacy Character Record from the First through Seventh Age (found in the Adventurer's Rulebook) or the newer Character Record found in the Cyber Age Hostilities rules expansion. You'll merely have to add a couple of skills (especially for Steampunk weapons) to account for pistols and steam-based machines, lore, etc.

A NOTE TO THE STORYTELLER

Waiting for you within these pages is a unique challenge: Steampunk Storytelling. People who sit down to play a Steampunk story are in for a treat, provided you've done your homework.

As the quote on the facing page relates, a steampunk milieu has a unique flavor of steam-powered machinery, airships, ticking gearwork, over-the-top eyewear, and robust romance amid submarine and skybound adventures. But there is more to it than that.

First, there is a steampunk style, and this style exists in beautiful clothing (Victorian era clothing is a favorite), music, architecture, product ads with impressive lettering, and, in our opinion the most important: novelty! Novelty of style is extremely important in this era, as competing scientists and entrepreneurs strive to outdo each other in impressive, monstrous, machinery that may or may not be exactly useful or efficient! When thinking up inventions of this sort, think steam steam steam (and more steam). Steam powers just about everything, even electrical current and lighting. Also think "Rube Goldberg" machines: using what you have available to make elaborate (oftentimes highly inefficient) machines.

Second, an Immortal Empires Steampunk Story is, at its foundation, different than all the other steampunk games out there. There is intrigue, backstabbing, political (perhaps imperial) ambitions, hidden (and forbidden) magic, plots, subplots, well-known heroes and even more beloved villains. You'll understand more of how an Immortal Empires Steampunk adventure stands apart from other steampunk games by the time

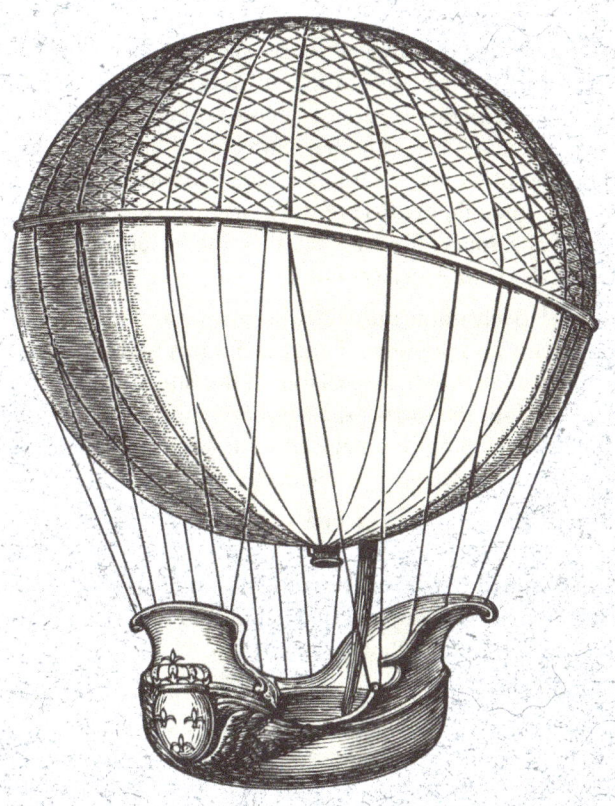

you're done with this booklet. It will be your job to ensure your players also understand and LOVE the distinguishing features.

Finally, whether you're going to have Immortals from the First through the Seventh or Eighth Ages (like Optimus, Maximillian, Furia Tarquinia, Ophelia Hadriana) is all up to you. There's a place for them, and it all makes sense.

In any case, the Storyteller section begins on page 39, but of course you should be familiar with everything in the Player section as well.

WHY STEAMPUNK?

Our Official Storyline is the reason we've included a Steampunk milieu, and the reason our Official Storyline includes it is because it's fun!

The Fourth Cataclysm

If you've been following the Official Storyline, you'd know that the extremely magical world of the Seventh Age lasts for only a couple of years, when suddenly the Great Plinth (and Aunt Julia (Evlain)) dies and departs the world. This event begins the transition into Dead Age.

The Dead Age comes into being as magic nearly completely dies out. The Ancient Races go into hiding because they are few in number compared to the hordes of Newborn (the Starborn follow the fate of the Ancient Races, shortly after). Of these, a small percentage becomes Immortal, and the rest are descendants propagating their races. At some point during the Dead Age, with the advent of larger seaworthy ships able to cross oceans, the other two continents (our Americas) are discovered, even though, because of the Remaking (the Third Cataclysm of the Sphere Tower war), they might look completely different than our Americas do.

The relatively nonmagical Newborn, now on equal keel with the Ancients and Starborn, hunt them down to destroy them, fearful lest they should be enslaved in the future should magic come back into the world. The Newborn continue on with the sciences, developing nonmagical machines, chemistry, architecture, structures, transportation, etc.

Things then develop as one would expect, based on our own world's history: hundreds of years of dark ages followed by some type of Renaissance, followed by hundreds of years of Enlightenment philosophies and nation-building, all of which leads to the Industrial Revolution.

In our game world, the Industrial Revolution transitions into the Computer Age (which is NOT the Cyber Age), then into the Nuclear Age...and then meets with the Fourth Cataclysm: Nuclear EMP World War. In this World War, only a couple of fiery nukes actually destroyed parts of the world; the majority of destruction is caused by EMP blasts (the major nations opted for EMP war instead of fiery nukes to actually save the planet from complete destruction).

This world war wipes out all the progress made with computers and technology, world-wide, relegating all nations' progress back to the pre-industrial era where mechanical machines were just beginning to come on the scene. This is because the normal sources of electricity have been wiped out with the war.

As nations start the rebuilding process (and remember, normal means of communication and transportation no longer exist, and so they are isolated, except for what horses survived), they turn to steam power, since it's the easiest technology that can be used to retrofit surviving machines.

Because of the lack of easy communications, different cultures will have vastly different designs for machines that accomplish similar tasks.

Under sinister re-direction from forces that arose out of the EMP anomalies, Steampunk does not evolve back into the innocent Computer Age, Nuclear Age and Space Age as one would expect. Instead, Steampunk evolves into a hostile Cyber Age followed by an escapist Galactic Age which is supposed to culminate in The Presidium coming back for their Star Legions.

The Rise of the Cabal

At the time of the world-wide EMP blasts, there were some Ancient and Starborn races (perhaps even a couple Immortals) centering on major plexuses in order to eke out a couple drops of magical tapping power (MTAP), as had been the survival custom ever since the inception of Dead Age.

Unfortunately, the EMPs reacted unpredictably with these major places of old, nearly forgotten, power, resulting in an anomaly (the Quickening) that killed nearly all the people who were centering there. Those who were unlucky enough to survive suffered monstrous physical and mental mutations.

Since all of the places of power (nexus/plexus) are connected with leylines, the survivors instantly became aware of each other as if having ONE MIND. None of them could be said to be the "Queen" or leader, but all of them together became aware of a superconscious they shared. This they called the Overmind. They became the appendages of the Overmind. They called themselves the Overmind: "We are Overmind."

Not having any need to travel to meet or share ideas, the Overmind quickly outpaced the rest of the world in developing technologies, stratagems and power bases.

Of primary importance to the Overmind was that it should grow. But, in spite of all the abductions, forced physical modifications, and even minor EMP pulse experiments on known places of power, they could not recreate the Quickening or add these abductees to their number.

This frustration of the Overmind's goal continues on through the Steampunk era to the Cyber Age where the Overmind achieves its first success in biotech implants that induct and enslave (and therefore artificially Quicken) the Cogs (a derogatory term they use for non-Quickened folks). Thus, the Overmind finally finds a way to grow itself.

In this respect, the Overmind is primarily responsible for creating the dark and dismal Age that is the Cyber Age.

Those who are lucky enough to escape the Overmind's experiments sputter forth claims about a "Cabal" of like-minded people who are attempting to enslave all of humanity to one "Overmind." At first, these people are just considered crazy (like the people in our world who claim to have been abducted by aliens/UFOs). But eventually, there are so many survivors describing similar circumstances that a cult legend starts to arouse societal fears.

Thus the Overmind will find it necessary to keep their true intentions Off Grid, but find it expedient to network their respective technology corporations On Grid. No one knows which corporations are run by the Overmind, at least until they are powerful enough to reveal a biotech device that enables people to go online with their brains on the OverNet, and thus be included secretly (unknown to the populace) and unknowingly subjugated to the Overmind. Even then, these corporations will deny accusations of being the Cabal as complete fabrications and "conspiracy theories" of nut-jobs.

At any time after the implant, however, the Overmind can artificially Quicken the person at will. Since there will be so many implants on the market, no one would know (at least initially) which implant was actually an Overmind one or not.

As people become artificially Quickened, they lose certain human aspirations and idiosyncrasies: a natural sense of humor, lack of affection, and human laziness, and so are able to be "detected" in some manner. The Overmind learns from their Quickened people getting discovered and killed that it's best to Quicken a whole town or city at the same time. They also try to humanize the Quickened with upgrades to their implants so that they will be less detectable among the masses.

The Overmind, being what it is, would never release a person once Quickened, so there is no "temporary Quickening" from which a person wakes. In fact, physical removal of the implant would likely cause the person to go crazy, as the Overmind will not lightly release its hold on the mind.

It may be that in the Cyber Age, the Ancient Races will be the only ones able to "magically" remove the implants safely.

The Cabal in the Steampunk Era

But in the Steampunk era, the Overmind mainly focuses on survival, conducting experiments only when assured their secrecy will be inviolate.

They welcome (and help spread) rumors of alien abductions, monsters and underground and underwater civilizations, as well as cities floating on the clouds: anything to desensitize the people to tales of fantastic adventure or murderous intrigue.

At least early on in Steampunk, the Cabal will consist only of the survivors of the EMP anomaly. They not only have the Overmind mentality, but also some physical mutation or deformity, which they will most likely keep hidden. They also might lose their ability to cast magic, or, perhaps, find that they can enhance their magical tapping power by drinking human blood, though the temporary boost to MTAP (from Blood Body Value (BBV)) would be extremely short-lived. These types of vampires would altogether be a new abomination in Steampunk fiction.

In any case, the Overmind uses all of its members together towards its goal, and it is wise enough, though perhaps not always patient enough, to continue its work without being wholly discovered and eradicated from the earth.

Finally, the Cabal will lead the way in Steampunk technology, either personally or by proxy (the non-Quickened). And since they KNOW that the Ancient Races have been hiding from the Newborn for centuries, and they KNOW where some of them live and their true identities, they will no doubt use this knowledge to their advantage. Though perhaps expedient at the time, this will also cause enmity between the Cabal and the Ancient Races who wish to remain free of the Cabal's influence.

So we have lots of material here for player Adventures. Your Storyteller may well have you going after some high-ranking Cabal member, or destroying a Cabal base of operations. Perhaps you'll start out as a slave and suddenly notice that the master of your house has started abducting people, and you'll have to find out why...

Your Storyteller may start your Adventure at any stage before, during, or after the Steampunk era and manipulate events, perhaps even Time Travel, to bring you into it. In addition, your Storyteller's milieu may be altogether different from the guidelines we've established in this booklet. With all that said, here's how we envision things.

Communications & Rebuilding

At the outset of the Steampunk era, those that have survived the EMP/Nuclear war will be focused on survival. The three basic necessities will be in short supply: food, clean water, and shelter will be hoarded and fought over.

Weapons and ammunitions of any sort will also be hoarded and treated just as important as food: highly guarded, rationed, and every bullet accounted for by the hierarchy survivors will arrange for themselves once they band together for protection.

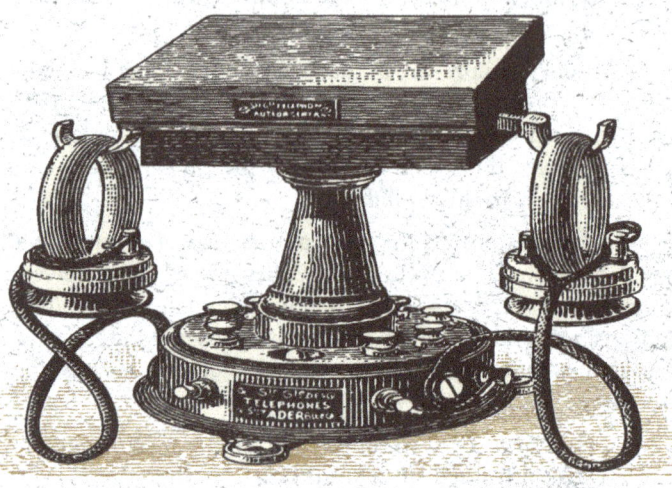

While other games/movies reinforce cliché post-apocalyptic stereotypes. the Immortal Empires Official Storyline parts ways with these stereotypes, so that instead of like-minded people gathering together to the exclusion of others (mean people with mean people, good people with good people, so everything becomes a good vs. evil paradigm), we recognize that people will band together based on proximity and need rather than good and bad.

With that said, every band of survivors will have several big badasses, geniuses, gardeners, pot smokers, selfish pricks, altruistic angels, doctors, etc., running the full gambit of personalities. They most likely will also have a bunch of computer programmers and other high-tech skilled people who have absolutely no value in the new society except to put their delicate hands to manual labor.

Of course, some bands will choose to use their aggregate talent to harm, rob, or subjugate others, and some will choose to help them and adopt them into their group. Some groups will view the new era as freedom from rules and institute every type of profligacy they can imagine; others will subscribe to the idea that the "End is Near" and start living lives that seek to avoid further judgment by the Powers, or by The One.

In short, then, you'll have to be ready for anything if you're thrust in a story where people can still taste the radioactive ions hanging in the air.

Communications will take some time to get back on line, and you can expect that even when they do, they will be local communications only. Even later on, when steam machines are able to power electricity, Steampunk telephones will likely only be networked to a few buildings within a highly guarded compound, leaving the masses to pass messages by courier or by homing pigeons and requests for help by signal fires.

There may indeed by some enclaves where survivors have moved into empty houses, buildings, or empty malls, prisons, or factories (that have machines that no longer work). The majority of survivors, however, will be on the move in search of safety, a steady food supply, and, if it can be, comfort.

While it may be that some vehicles and gasoline survived the EMP/Nukes, these will be very rare, and eventually end up in the hands of the very powerful. The vast majority of machines will have to be retrofitted with steam power contraptions that provide enough energy to turn the gears, so to speak.

As people move from survival to rebuilding, they'll start to settle down in a house of their own, and begin to contribute to a community to farm, build, and look to the needs a community has.

The exact nature of the transition to full-blown Steampunk is for your Storyteller to decide. After this section, we will describe the Steampunk milieu in full stride, far after any transition, and far before any fading into Cyber Age Hostilities.

So we dedicate here just these few lines to the transition from the Steampunk era to the Cyber Age. With certain clandestine guidance from the Cabal, Steampunk technology becomes more advanced, smaller and efficient. A new computer age is born, but one that merges technology and biology.

Technology & Steam

Steam power, though oftentimes massive and heavy and notoriously consuming (you need to feed a fire and you need to keep water above the fire) can provide a great deal of energy to lift, push, turn, pull, and inflate just about any machine you can think of: from retrofitted automobiles to steam powered sewing machines.

Steampunk dwellings and businesses, then, will always have four parts to a steam system: [1] fire supply area, [2] boiling cistern, [3] the machine proper, and [4] refuse area (to store wood ashes, coal fly and bottom ash, boiler slag, and any other resultant waste that would arise from whatever was burned to heat the water to steam).

The fire supply area consists of the fire itself and the fire's fuel, whether that be wood, coal, or anything else that will burn without exploding. The fire chamber will need intake and exhaust ventilation, and will need to be placed under or close to the boiling cistern which should be made of a material that transfers heat well (iron/steel, which is what makes these machines so massive and heavy!).

The boiling cistern can be small or large, depending on the purpose, and will require a constant water supply for as long as the machine will be running. It is entirely possible that the machine therefore have a water tank (not heated) that feeds into a smaller boiling cistern so that the machine will produce steam more quickly upon start up. The more advanced steam machines will aim to recycle steam back to the cooler water tank in order to be used over again. But most of the machines will have leaky pipes that blow out steam from their seams, drip hot water, and make a lot of noise!

The machine proper will probably have a variety of pipes that bring the steam past finned flywheels that are attached to gears that employ simple machines: inclining planes, levers, wedges, wheel and axles, pulleys, and screws (that pull together or push apart, depending on the screw threading).

We challenge you to think of a machine that could not be powered by steam. In fact, we think that steam could be used for powering virtually anything, if size of the machine did not matter.

Electricity & Steam

So what about electricity? Survivors will still remember the basic necessity for creating electricity: mechanical energy must be used to rotate coils of copper wire between poles of a magnet. In fact, such a simple generator (Michael Faraday generator), could be turned by hand to create a current. Of course it is much more efficient to create a turbine and let something besides your hand turn the generator: falling water (like a waterfall), wind, or, yup, you guessed it: steam!

Power lines connected to the generator then carry the electric current wherever it is needed. But since much was destroyed, even these small electrical devices must be remade, and to do that, people will need bigger machines to do the mining, screwing, welding, etc.

But in a Steampunk game well on its way in the era, most of this is already done, and people can start taking luxuries (like electricity) for granted once more, as well as other things: plumbing, mechanical vehicles/transportation, and perhaps even refrigeration, although that might be a luxury too costly for the lowly masses.

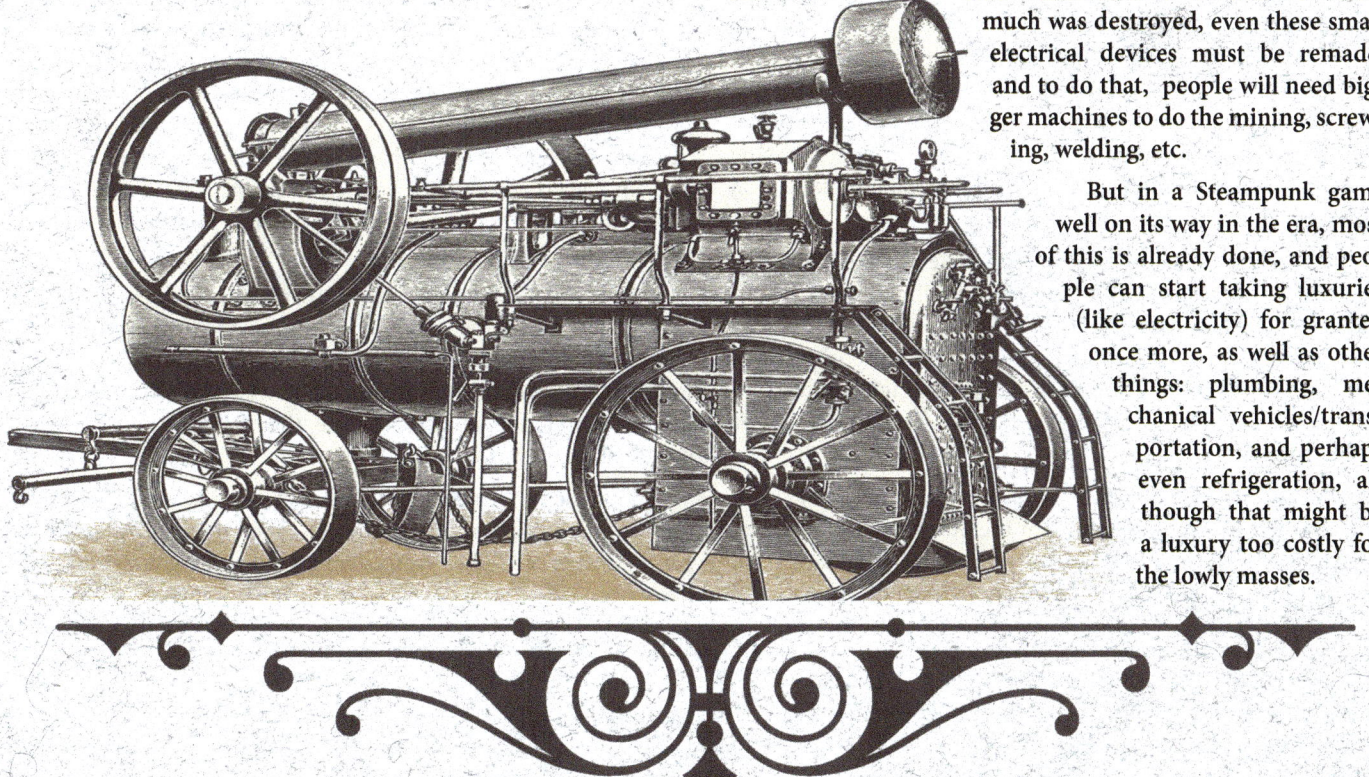

Governments & Citizenry

After the catastrophe, people try to rebuild according to what is familiar to them, since that seems safe (even though it was the governments in the first place that led to the catastrophe!). So, we imagine that our Steampunk era will have local leadership (mayors), but that it would take some time before people subscribe to regional governments again, even though there will be some who advocate (or attempt to force) that allegiance.

And because of the lack of far-spread communications and travel, local leaders will have much more power than a so-called regional governor anyway. Hence, towns will each have their own personality and social hierarchy of gossips, activities, parties, love affairs, and extravagance, and, let's not forget exclusive high society memberships, depending on the deportment of the town's Mayor, who would either be chosen and respected by the people or would have appointed him/herself the head honcho and rules through intimidation and fear.

Unless you're traveling from another Age into this era, you'll most likely be part of a town system, or at least know about a town near where you live if you're a country folk. Either way, you'll be expected to contribute something to helping the town grow. And even strangers passing through the town might be "taxed," and thereafter looked upon with suspicion until they've left the area.

But inventors and traveling sales people can easily win the hearts of a town, especially if they have something new to show, which is something you may want to keep in mind. Traders are also welcome, as long as they have something useful to trade and don't try to rob the people blind for "miracle potions" although there will be plenty of charlatans with whom you'll be able to mingle.

As such, the idea of citizenry to most is a "far-away" concept that really has no meaning in the Steampunk era. Everyone knows that any national identity before has been destroyed and that there is no army powerful enough to enforce national boundaries or national identities anyway. No, people are quite contented to identify with a town, and let that be enough.

The vast freedoms they enjoy now are a welcome change from the millions of oppressive laws their former governments imposed upon them under threat of imprisonment or death.

In fact, it could be said that Steampunk citizens are hostile to the idea of nation-building, desiring to preserve their newfound freedoms from the tyranny ALL governmental systems eventually impose.

Geography

If you'll be using our Official Storyline, the geography of the Roman Empire, Africa, Asia and Europe has changed to be nearly unrecognizable on account of He Who Stands Alone's Remaking with the power of the Sphere Towers (oh, and by the way, the Marunes will still be in an Immortal Empires Steampunk story...somewhere, so be on your guard!).

As for the western hemisphere, Immortal Empires is purposely leaving it undefined so that Storytellers can develop whatever they want there: the American continents, a massive sprawl of island-continents, ocean only (like a Water world), whatever. Perhaps it's a completely new civilization with new Philosophies like Christianity or Islam or Buddhism or what-have-you (and perhaps they war with each other completely oblivious and unconcerned with the eastern hemisphere). It is entirely up to the Storyteller as to what the western hemisphere holds (if anything), and we will not encroach on their space.

But as for our Remade maps (in the Storyteller's Codex), they can certainly be used for Steampunk, with some small changes. For example, the floating island of Rhodes will have fallen into the sea since magic died; likewise, Arkadia has dried up and is no longer a magical place, the magical portals to Faerie Realm having long since been shut.

Additionally, there will be huge wastelands of radioactive fallout that become more deadly the closer one gets to ground zero. So, take care where you go and what water you drink.

The Grid and Off the Grid

Even though there will be great benefit to abiding in a town and being known to everyone in the town, i.e., ON the Grid (grid meaning plugged in to society in a way that one is known as a member of that society), there will still be those who do not fit in to any of the societies that spring up after the Fourth Cataclysm.

These people (and not all of them necessarily have to be criminals, mind you) then live outside of a societal system, apart from any town or society, their true identities hidden. They avoid the rules others have made, they pay no taxes, and in fact might have a currency all their own. These people are said to live OFF the grid.

Most of those off the grid, at least initially, will be so because they are criminals as defined by their localities, being chased by the grasping claws of justice of one town or another. These individuals would be off the grid by necessity.

But there are those who choose to be off the grid so as to conduct their lives as they see fit without authoritative intrusion into their plans. They do not care to have an on-grid identity. They are akin to "mountain men" or "hermits" and are skilled enough to be self-sustainable.

Then there is the truly sinister and duplicitous person who lives both on grid and off grid. She seems to have a great social standing as one of the Madams of High Society in Steamtown, but off grid, she is an assassin for hire, dealing solely in shares of stock in promising machinery companies. On grid, she is Lady Martha Clare of Beaumont, a community leader who is notorious for falling in love with other women's husbands, but who is so rich she still has all the Ladies come to her tea parties (even though many of them hate her).

Off grid, however, she is known only as The Clipper, and it is impossible to meet The Clipper or see *him*, because he's off grid. In fact, the only way you might even be able to hire The Clipper is to put a wanted ad in one of the local papers servicing Beaumont, Remont, Tellmont, and Birdsmont. But to do that, you'd have to know exactly how to word it by being a member of the High Society gossips (who would also gossip that you were in fact looking for an assassin for some reason... perhaps even to knock off that adulteress Lady Martha Clare). Don't worry, it's just gossip. But The Clipper will find you, so long as you placed a frown in the ad and worded it correctly, so the urban legend would have it. And if you're willing to pay his price, he'll do what you're too busy (or too cowardly) to do yourself.

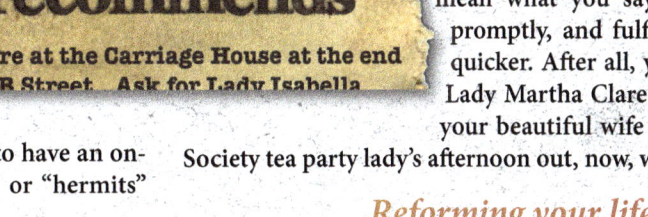

Eventually, the world of OFF GRID will become a seedy haven for all manner of society rejects, where there's a price for every vice and where no laws prohibit them.

But, this is also a dangerous underground where reputation is paramount. Here, all you have is your word. Break it, and someone will break you. There won't be any constable or Mayor to run to for protection, so you'd better say what you mean and mean what you say, pay your debts promptly, and fulfill your jobs even quicker. After all, you wouldn't want Lady Martha Clare suddenly inviting your beautiful wife to a gossipy High Society tea party lady's afternoon out, now, would you?

Reforming your life

Just because you're off the grid doesn't mean you have to stay off the grid. There are plenty of ex-off-grid or special interest groups that will help you to become a slave of society again, even helping you to avoid any lawful punishments that otherwise would have deterred you, provided, of course, you swear loyalty to them. They might even appreciate some of your off grid skills if you put them to use for the group.

Yes, we're talking about Secret Societies. They're not exactly off grid, as they're above such seedy and filthy (and dangerous) living. The men and women who take part of secret societies wouldn't be caught dead in a dark alley somewhere negotiating a price for something. Nope. That's what you'll be for. You'll take care of the situation yourself. Just don't get caught, because they won't know you if you are.

New Vocations

What would an essential expansion be without new Player Character Vocations? We've added eight Vocations:

Calling	Steampunk Vocation
Politician	Aristocrat
Scholar	Inventor
Scholar	Chemist
Rogue	Charlatan
Rogue	Merchant
Rogue	Explorer
Warrior	Constable
Guardian	Preacher

These new Vocations in Steampunk will have considerably fewer perks than new Vocations in either the Adventurer's Rulebook or the Cyber Age Hostilities rules expansion. The reason for this is that we view them more as "playing styles" that the Newborn (and Steampunk) societies will have, Vocations that the Ancient Races must "adopt" in order to remain hidden.

Steampunk heroes, by virtue of the entire broken era, are considerably less powerful than those legendary heroes of the First through Seventh Ages (and also those from the future, where abilities will be greatly enhanced by technology). You'll have to rely more on your wits to survive (much like the Dead Age). If your character is not of the past or the future, but just a normal Steampunk citizen, you'll have a most challenging time (that can be very rewarding) in making your character legendary. In the Storyteller section of this book, we recommend some bonuses for non-Ancient Race/non-Cyber Steampunk ORank increases.

If your Storyteller is running the type of story where you'll be an Ancient Race descendant/immortal, then of course all Vocations (including a magic throwing Scholar) are good choices, because you'll have to run them under the "guise" of the new Vocations anyway lest you come under suspicion by your communities of being an Ancient Race (whom they may attempt to kill on sight).

The Aristocrat

Networking, respect, and uppity living, characterized by "learnéd" philosophical, scientific, and even metaphysical, talk and public ridicule for the men; gossip and social ostracism for the women. Of course, the negative aspects are more hidden for those aristocrats that have achieved influence, which is of great important to the Gentleman/Lady.

In order to be influential, they strive for recognition and preeminence in their social circles, the main Steampunk social circle being "High Society," an exclusive clique consisting of all the "important" people of a town or group of small towns. This clique just about always includes the town's Mayor (and spouse), the Chief Constable (and spouse), and prominent bachelors and damsels of means.

High Society Steampunk culture celebrates not so much luxurious excess, but the idea that Ladies and Gentlemen are high-

ly educated and therefore enjoy the finer things (luxuries) of life by nature, not by hard work to get those things. Hard work characterizes the uneducated masses, not High Society.

Here's an example of a typical conversation among women:

non-High Society Guest: "Your home is beautiful — and the carpet on the stairs! Is that woven from black lambswool?"

High Society Home Owner: "Naturally."

High Society Guest: "Surely, you did not buy that carpet from the Charlatan that was hanged last month for selling rat meat as a delicacy, and then harvesting their furs for various rugs. Your carpet looks vaguely familiar in that respect."

High Society Home Owner: "I should say not! My carpet is from the one and only Elias Bellbrook."

non-High Society Guest: "The Inventor?"

High Society Guest: *Walks over to feel the carpet.* "You don't say...I am quite impressed with his weaving machines he's steamed to life. Well, rat or lamb. It fits your style.

High Society Home Owner: "Thank you. Perhaps some day that husband of yours will deign to carpet your stairs with soft beauty instead of fritter away your fortunes on those toys he calls machines."

In the above conversation, the non-High Society Guest might be too uneducated to appreciate the subtle sparring going on between the High Society gossips. At the same time, the Ladies are too educated to actually take offense at what the other says, seeing the whole conversation as an exercise in wit, an opportunity to show who can control the conversation with the art of banter.

As in all Steampunk, how one dresses herself is of extreme importance, for the clothing immediately lets another know how you expect to be treated. For High Society ladies and gentlemen, dresses and suits, top hats, overcoats, luxurious furs, capes and cleavage-showing corsets, all with expensive cufflinks or jewels and other fine buttons.

Aristocrats choose to dress either as Dandy or Femme Fatale. They smoke (tobacco, among other weeds), and often have overly long fag holders.

All Aristocrats gain the following bonuses at character creation for free:

+1 INT	Social Trait +1: Positive House Reputation
+1 INS	Social Trait +1: Very Minor Inheritance II
1 Fine Horse	1 Small Townhouse in the wealthier section of town

They also receive bonuses based on ORank:

ORank	Boon
3	Social Trait +3: Wealthy
5	Social Trait +3: Social Manipulator
7	Social Trait +3: Moderate Inheritance I
10	Social Trait +3: Moderate Inheritance II (MenH items)

Playing an Aristocrat in the Steampunk era can be quite fun if you're the witty type and can quip with the best of them. They are also quite useful in an adventuring party because of their High Society contacts, wealth, their ability to host everyone in their homes, and, finally, their educated air of superiority.

The Inventor

One of the most interesting yet challenging Vocations you can play is the Inventor. Inventors are naturally inquisitive about every aspect of machine lore, past and present, have huge imaginations and even larger egos.

Inventors can specialize in different fields from being just a general mechanic, and can become an aviator, a locomotive engineer, or even a dirigible captain who prefers to submerge in his own invention rather than entrust his life to the paltry designs of some inferior inventor.

Intelligent enough to see through the useless banter of the aristocrats, the Inventor abandons an eclectic education in favor of cogs, steam and wires. For this reason, although highly respected should his inventions gain popularity, the Inventor is not looked upon as a highly educated person. Thus while certainly able to be invited to a High Society function, he would never be a regular, especially if another Inventor comes along with a new and exciting machine that sucks up all the air in the room, so to speak. In fact, competition among inventors can get bloody.

The Inventor sees others, even Aristocrats, as ignoramuses, and has little patience in trying to explain his thought processes or the functioning inner workings of his inventions. "Don't touch that!" is his favorite reprimand. Of course, he knows he needs to temper his temper with enough civility in order to get the loan from the Aristocrats funding the next experimental design.

Inventors do not always follow the laws, seeing the science of invention as much more important than superficial "kind" society norms and etiquette. Unfortunately, this attitude has served to only force some great inventors into hiding, being labeled as "mad scientists" and their work characterized as dangerous to mankind's well-being. Doctor Frankenstein, Josef Mengele (Nazi), Captain Nemo, Jose Delgado (as Overmind associate), Sergei Brukhonenko (early life support machines), and Nikola Tesla would be great Steampunk-worthy examples.

All Inventors gain the following bonuses at character creation for free:

+2 INT	Social Trait +1: Powerbase Begun
Small Laboratory	Social Trait +1: Tentative Allies II
1 Steam Engine	1 covered, motorized vehicle that can carry 1/2 ton

They also receive bonuses based on ORank:

ORank	Boon
3	Social Trait +3: Influential Buddy
5	Social Trait +3: Minor Allies II (High Society)
7	Social Trait +3: Affiliated
10	Social Trait +3/-3: Well-known / Publicly Ousted*

* If your actions as an Inventor have demanded that you were Publicly Ousted, it should not be without some great gain your sacrifice has achieved. Storyteller: Make it so!

Playing an Inventor in the Steampunk era is a challenging one, but one that can be of great service to your fellow players: you can bring much to the table (without having to pay another inventor for a machine you need), provided they can get the parts you need.

The Chemist

A cousin of the Inventor, the Chemist has a love for the nearly magical reactions that precise mixing of a variety of substances can have. S/he is an expert in minerals, acids, explosive reactions, salves, medicines, poisons, and eventually vaccines. As such, Chemists utterly despise charlatans who engender public mistrust of the true chemist profession. They would like nothing more than for the charlatan to suffer by imbibing a concoction of a real chemist.

Perhaps that's why, when chemists find that they can barely rub two coins together in their chosen career, they turn to entertaining the masses as magicians, creating fireworks and other dazzling effects for the uneducated to "ooh and ahh" at. While it could be an annoying distraction from their true love, performing thus, and traveling from one city to another, suits their constant search for more, and new, plants and other substances with which to further their chemical experimentations. It should be said, however, that some chemists have made a successful living as apothecaries.

Aristocrats find chemists quite entertaining at dinner parties, not just for their magical tricks, but on account of their vast knowledge of edible and poisonous mushrooms, intoxicating plant leaves, poisonous fruits, and even what enemas are made from (constipation is a major problem among some aristocrats). While perhaps necessary, most chemists loathe playing the magician to aristocrats, and would much rather spend their time in the lab.

Charlatans steer clear of chemists, for fear of being exposed (or worse). Inventors are indifferent, except when they might need a chemical power boost for their machines. Constables are wary of chemists as potential poisoners. And Merchants are all about using a chemist to make them rich (as they take large cuts of the sales themselves): some try to partner with chemists

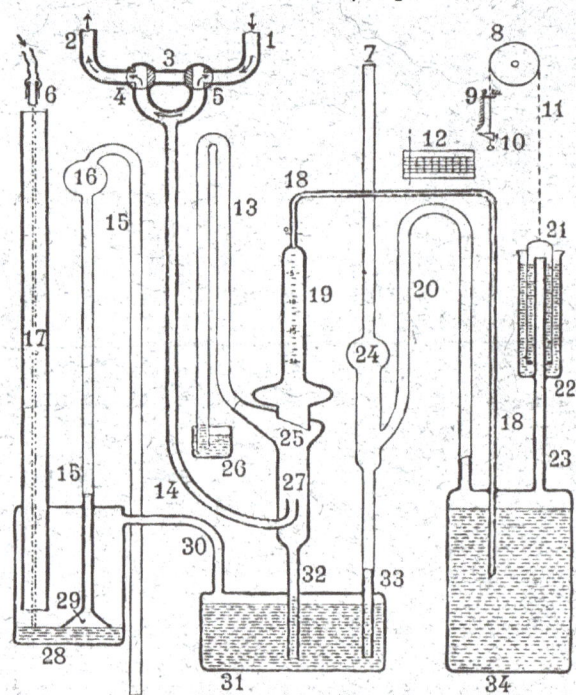

for a worthy On Grid product; others try to offer prohibited alchemical products on the black markets (Off Grid) without getting caught by the Mayors who have outlawed them.

Like Inventors, Chemists can become "mad scientists," and are much likely to be much more feared than their ostracized cousins, since they can do so much more damage! More fear means more earnestly hunted by the powers that be.

Of paramount importance to a Chemist is her laboratory; it must be salvaged at all costs, especially if she has not journaled a certain process or result yet. And that brings us to another

cherished item a Chemist has: her journal. Her discoveries, measurements, lab constructions, reaction temperatures, etc., will be neatly recorded therein, and it is highly secret, likely even written in code. Because this journal can be worth so much money to another Chemist or treacherous Saleslady, this is another reason many Chemists opt to guise themselves as some other profession (magician, physician, etc.).

If you're a person of few words, the Chemist might be a great choice for your character. After all, you're more interested in results and how you can help (hurt?) a populace with your concoctions. Let the role of convincing them verbally reside with the loquacious Charlatans. Your results will speak loudly enough for themselves.

All Chemists gain the following bonuses at character creation for free:

+2 INS	Learning Trait +1: Apothecary, Metallurgy, Biology
Small Laboratory	Social Trait +1: Toga Virilis (pertaining to alchemy)
Covered Wagon	Physical Trait +1: Poison Tolerance

They also receive bonuses based on ORank:

ORank	Boon
3	Social Trait +1: E.F. Hutton Syndrome
5	Social Trait +1: Secret Lover (High Society)
7	Social Trait +5: Get Out of Jail Free Card
10	Social Trait +5/-5: Well-Connected / Fugitive*

* If your actions as a Chemist have demanded that you had to become a Fugitive, it should not be without some great gain your sacrifice has achieved. Storyteller: Make it so!

Playing a Steampunk Chemist can yield your character great power for good or for ill. Which path will you choose? And will your fellow players turn on you or join you in your conquest?

The Charlatan

Grandiloquent speech places the Charlatan above the Merchant and mere Chemist); in the Charlatan's mind he is far their superior, a harbinger delivering a popular product to the weak, fearful and infirm among us: peace of mind.

The Charlatan's main asset is not the Miracle Elixir he's stumbled upon; it is not the ornate double-bladed falchion swinging at his side by which he proposes to vanquish the town's monsters; it is not even his significant other with whom he beds down at night, though she is without doubt endowed

with distracting main assets of her own; no, a Charlatan's main assets is his tongue, for by the power thereof, he is able to replace suspicion with hope, fear with confidence, and his empty pockets with coin.

A professional Monster Hunter, the Charlatan dares to venture where more feeble men dare not (he's careful not to let on that the monstrous occurrences have been incited by the secret retinue in his employ, and of course disavows all knowledge of

them should they ever be found out as perpetuating the hoax). Yes, for a meager sum, a small sacrifice, really, from each town's citizen, he'll vanquish the beast and show bloody proof of it to boot.

In the meanwhile, women and children and delicate men should avail themselves of his soothing miracle elixirs such as absinthe, cocaine syrup, and honey medicine (with just a touch of alcohol to make it believable).

Far from what his detractors, those shameful practitioners of Chemistry, might say, the Charlatan is no purveyor of false cures or scandalous hoaxes, nor does he proffer mephitic prophylactics (perhaps occasionally, to be honest, and only when the ailment makes it medically necessary).

But there is no falsehood in what he claims. For what he advertises, he sells; the medium used is of far less importance. Do

his elixirs dull the pain? Absolutely. Do they calm the nerves? Without doubt! (Never mind their addictive nature.) And has the terror of the monster been eradicated from the land? Yes, it has been either chased off (his accomplices are getting drunk in the tavern) or another animal has become its scapegoat, whose bloody entrails are proof of the Charlatan's trustworthiness. But all in all, peace of mind and security are restored to each individual who may have been suffering before the Charlatan's gracious appearance.

If you have the gift of gab, then perhaps the Charlatan is the right character Vocation for you. Of course, Charlatans don't call themselves charlatans! They go by ever more exalted (and superfluous) names akin to the multiplicitous titles and cognomens of old. For example:

Zenas the Miracle Worker: Monster Hunter Extraordinaire!
Percipicles the Great and Mighty Dragon Slayer
Pharos the Wise: Apothecary of Exotic Cures

are just three great names that have floated about like angels exacting punishment on wrongdoers, detractors, and beasts that have plagued countless upstanding townsfolk from the west sea to the east sea.

Some Charlatans engage monsters in the sea themselves, calling upon a great Inventor with whom to collude (and share some of the spoils for a quiet tongue). Just let the Charlatan do the talking, and everything will be fine.

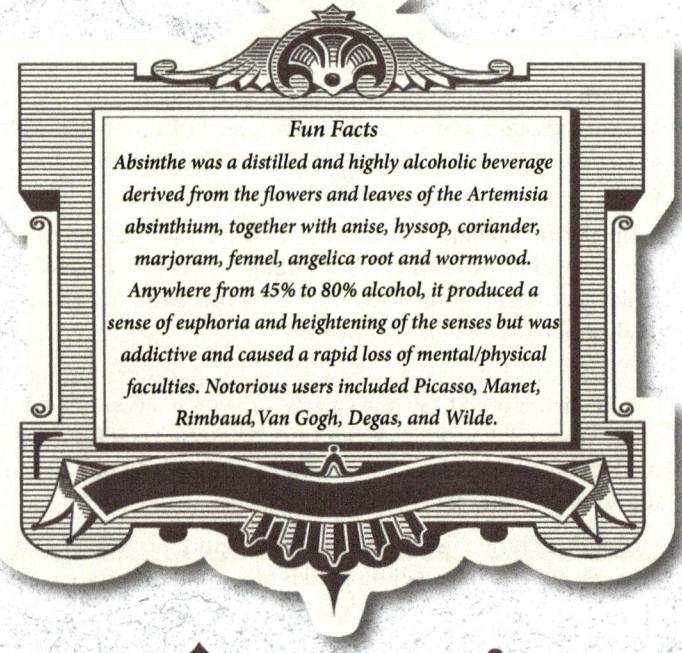

Fun Facts

Absinthe was a distilled and highly alcoholic beverage derived from the flowers and leaves of the Artemisia absinthium, together with anise, hyssop, coriander, marjoram, fennel, angelica root and wormwood. Anywhere from 45% to 80% alcohol, it produced a sense of euphoria and heightening of the senses but was addictive and caused a rapid loss of mental/physical faculties. Notorious users included Picasso, Manet, Rimbaud, Van Gogh, Degas, and Wilde.

All Charlatans gain the following bonuses at character creation for free:

+2 EMP	Social Trait +1: Confidant
1 Horse	Social Trait +1: Gang Leader
Loyal Servant*	Horse-drawn or steampowered wagon/covered vehicle

They also receive bonuses based on ORank:

ORank	Boon
3	Social Trait +3: Fixer Apprentice
5	Social Trait +3: Talented Sycophant
7	Social Trait +3: Get Out of Jail Free Card
10	Social Trait +3/-3: Affiliated / Hunted by Overzealous Sheriff (Constable)**

* This is purely optional. The loyal servant can be a wife or husband, son/daughter, or someone you rescued from a dire situation and owes you a great deal.

** If your actions as a Charlatan have demanded that you had to be Hunted by an Overzealous Constable, it should not be without some great gain your sacrifice has achieved. Storyteller: Make it so!

Playing a Steampunk Charlatan will certainly be one of the most rewarding experiences you'll ever have. You'll run circles around the Storyteller's ornery Personalities she's placed in the story, and gain a bunch of laughs from the other players, all the while swindling some coin for yourself.

The Merchant

Not one to mince words, the Merchant takes business very seriously. He's naturally knowledgeable on the current events of a large area on account of his travels in search of trade and new partnerships.

The Merchant endeavors to build his brand, to become the preferred supplier of a spectrum of products to both Aristocrats and the bourgeoisie alike. As for the poor, the Merchant will have *something* available; after all, he doesn't want to be hated or talked about badly, and even the poor might have some coin or something useful to trade, even if it's helpful information that will give the Merchant leverage for making his next deal.

Sometimes the Merchant starts out as a door-to-door salesman, or perhaps a traveling trader, or even own a general store. Sadly, he's often mistaken for a charlatan and since he does not have the loquacious gifts most charlatans have comes under

suspicion by the very people with whom he's trying to build a business friendship! But if he can gain the confidence of at least one influential person, especially a High Society uppity who becomes a patron, he'll be on the road to success.

Whether starting solo or with a couple partners, the Merchant is always trying to grow his trade network. So, he'll bend over backwards to make sure that his customers are happy, his patrons are getting wealthier, and his competition insignificant.

To that end, he'll try to play by the rules, even though he knows others don't. But if you push him into a corner, where he has to visit a judge (or worse: venture off grid) to teach you a lesson, watch your back! The Merchant knows many people in many towns, from farmers and small-time suppliers to powerful Aristocrats and Mayors for whom he had done several favors, not to mention other Merchants and even Constables he's impressed along the way by greasing their wheels with free meals or candy for their children.

Now, we should say also that the Merchant is perfectly capable of building a brand of just ONE main product instead of several (or dozens of) products. On this path, he might become a specialist in one product, sell all related items to that product and even have a couple of machines he's acquired that help him diagnose the customer that needs that product. A perfect example of this is the above image, in which Dr. Johnson sells glasses, optical lenses and magic lanterns. In any case, the Merchant is always a very active person, usually in good shape.

All Merchants gain the following bonuses at character creation for free:

+1 EMP	Social Trait +1: Fence
+1 INT	Social Trait +1: Tentative Allies I (High Society)
1 Horse	Social Trait +1: VERY Minor Inheritance II

They also receive bonuses based on ORank:

ORank	Boon
3	Learning Trait +1: SK:Trade Lore, SK:Savvy, Regional
5	Social Trait +5: Fixer
7	Physical Trait +1: Healthy
10	Social Trait +5: Business Tycoon

Playing a Steampunk Merchant can result in great wealth and a vast network you can use to your advantage. But beware, there is also the other up-and-comer who wants to take over your turf, and you'll always have to deal with Charlatans trying to steal your customers away with addictive magical cures that seem to put your products to shame.

The Constable

Military training and zeal for upholding a town's laws, no matter how oppressive or one-sided, make the Constable stand out among his peers. She knows right well who makes the rules, and it's the same ones who need protection from those who don't.

In the Steampunk era, a Constable is not an officer of the peace, nor is she a servant of the public. Constables exist only to ensure that High Society is protected and remains privileged, even though most Constables never ascend to High Society at all. Only the Chief Constable, who's buddy-buddy with the Mayor is accepted into their circles. But the others know that perhaps someday, with enough loyal ass kissing and public displays of loyalty (you know, upholding the "law"), that some day their ship will come in (or perhaps their secret lover in High Society will be the next Mayor and choose them as Chief Constable).

Thus, a Constable is not about to come running every time some commoner yells "Help" or "Thief" or "Rape." Not unless the yeller is someone important, anyway. Of course, they're always on the lookout for con artists trying to suck High Society in to their schemes, but might turn a blind eye if the con artist is in league with one of the Constable's High Society contacts.

Perhaps only outdone in political intrigue by Aristocrats themselves, Constables navigate these dangerous waters with cautious ambition, for it is not unheard of for the Chief Constable to eventually become Mayor! True, there might be the altrustic Constable somewhere, but she would soon learn who her masters were, were she to try to arrest one of them. Hence, the attitude and general atmosphere of the town is primarily

to blame for the Constable's deportment, including his overall level of corruption. It certainly would be a challenge in any Steampunk setting for a Constable to avoid corruption altogether and still achieve success. We'll leave that to you, if you dare to try.

On having to be roused to settle a public dispute or fight among the commoners, a Constable is likely to throw the whole lot of them in jail, and let the judge (or the Mayor) sort it out. But occasionally, one will get a hair up her ass and hunt down an individual who crossed her in some way, High Society mem-

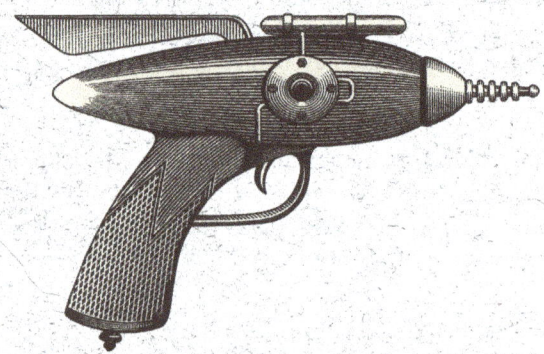

bership notwithstanding. If you mistreat a Constable, no matter what your social standing, she'll find some way to bring you down.

Some wealthy Mayors invest a great deal in their Constable force, paying renown Inventors for special weapons only their Constables have. Take, for instance, the Steam powered electricity gun above. It attaches to a steam source at the bottom of the stock, and so long as that steam source tube feeds it steam, the turbine can turn and shoot out enough electricity to stop a man (or woman) cold. Without the steam hose, however, it's only useful for about five minutes after being disconnected, and then only for one short use. Still, it's a pretty nice thing to have, right? Especially if you're called to defend the Mayor against another Mayor's hostilities.

Some towns don't let women become Constables, citing the vulnerability of the fairer sex; furthermore, a Constable rarely has authority outside of his or her Mayor's zone of control. It should be noted that in Steampunk, a Constable's authority is in all cases a mere illusion, unless s/he has the ready equipment, fighting skill, and/or extra soldiers to enforce the law. Many a Constable have ended up face down in a rainy ditch for overstepping their office. It will be your task to make sure you

never become one of those.

Sometimes, Constables grow tired of the political intrigue and abandon dreams of High Society luxury, using their considerable military and combat skills to become Explorers, or bodyguards for Explorers and Merchants, hit men off grid (if there's substantial coin involved), or some other type of mercenary. Whatever his/her path, s/he demands respect wherever their travels take them (unless, of course, it's back home where they'll once again be under the uppity noses of their High Society masters).

All Constables gain the following bonuses at character creation for free:

+1 PHQ	Physical Trait +1: Thick Skin I or II
+1 AGL	Physical Trait +1: Tough
+1 COR	Physical Trait +1: Agile

They also receive bonuses based on ORank:

ORank	Boon
3	Physical Trait +3: Cornfed Body Type
5	Physical Trait +3: Physical Resistance
7*	Social Trait +3: Military Rank / Minor Allies II
10*	Social Trait +3/-3: High Society Marriage / Dignitas Enhancement / Affiliated / Hunted by Small-time Criminals / Hated by the Plebs / Hunted by Vigilante

* Constables get to choose ONE of these Boons at ORank7 and ORank10, depending on how his/her Story is going.

If you're the type that prefers political intrigue and putting your weapon where your mouth is when you're not kissing ass (or plotting to take over the town), then this is the right Vocation for you. Smart Constables just might end up being Mayor some day. Are you up to the challenge?

The Preacher

Got your convictions? Should others believe the way you do? Does the town just need to hear your warnings? Do you have the well-being of every individual at heart?

Or, do you really just want them to follow you off a cliff for your own ego (or for your own pocket book! After all, when everyone is keeled over for having drunk the cool-aid, you can move into the Mayor's mansion and start your own town with your own rules).

Either way, the Preacher has something to say, although not

much about his/her true motives for saying it. Appearing to be the moral compass helping all societies avoid backsliding to the bad behavior that led to the Fourth Cataclysm, the Preacher reaches into people's emotions to gain their trust and respect.

Servant of the poor. Supplicant of the rich. Rebuker of the indifferent. The Preacher uses all his skills to hold society together, and to keep everyone from each other's throats! (At least until such time he sees fit to stir up his congregation(s) for a "moral" march against: tyranny, or corruption, or you-name-it, because you never know the true motives of a Preacher until he makes his move.

Because so many confide in the Preacher, he knows many secrets, and he knows how to turn those secrets against you, quietly and patiently fomenting dissent until just the right time. Of course, we're talking here about an evil Preacher (like Stephen King's wicked shop owner in "Needful Things"). What about a good Preacher?

A good Preacher is definitely a welcome addition to any town and are oft hired by Aristocrats as tutors for their children. They can also be very useful to an adventuring party, because people just naturally trust Preachers. For that reason, she's a great asset when you need information about a populace or person. She knows how to validate people, give them dignity, and unite them to a common cause, like making an extra effort to feed the poor, or come together if there's a monster afoot, or helping to raise money so that the town can hire an Inventor to come and improve their quality of life.

As idealistic as the Preacher may be, s/he is tempted each day with so many evils that it might be difficult for them to remain true to their convictions; after all, knowing the secrets of so many is a great burden to carry. It might be better to use those secrets to one's advantage, perhaps?

Mind you, a Preacher does not have to preach about religion or Philosophy, but whatever he preaches about, it's bound to make some enemies somewhere (especially with other Preachers entertaining opposing convictions or more ambitious goals).

It could be said that a very powerful alliance could be made between a Preacher and a Charlatan. If that were to happen, so long as the Charlatan, for all appearances, abode in the Preacher's rigid code of conduct, no town would be safe!

Role-playing a Preacher can be quite challenging, especially when you have to make up your own doctrine. But it gets a little easier once (if ever) you discover what the Overmind are up to; it is then when all towns everywhere will need to hear your genuine concern for their well-being. You might be so effective as to be recruited by the Overmind itself, if you're that wishy washy on what you believe.

All Preachers gain the following bonuses at character creation for free:

+3 EMP	Social Trait +1: Life of the Party
	Social Trait +1: Bard
	Social Trait +1: Confidant

They also receive bonuses based on ORank:

ORank	Boon
3	Learning Trait +3: Wonder Worker
5	Physical Trait +3: Sensual
7	Social Trait +5: Social Genius
10*	Social Trait +3/-3: Plebeian Favorite / High Society Marriage / Hated by the Plebs / Jilted by Secret Lover

* If your actions as a Preacher have demanded that you had to be Hated by the Plebs (Commoners) or Jilted by a Secret Lover, it should not be without some great gain your sacrifice has achieved. Storyteller: Make it so!

If you want to manipulate the townspeople into becoming your followers, whether by hook or crook (or just by being a great person), then this is the right Vocation for you. After all the people are under your spell, you'd be wise to be wary of the Mayor who knows you have his/her people's loyalties.

The Explorer a.k.a. Scavenger

The Steampunk Explorer has nothing in common with Lewis & Clark, in that the latter explored unknown expanses. More akin to a vagabond, the Steampunk Explorer investigates charted but dangerous ruins. S/he is tough and has the skills to survive in the destroyed cities and wildernesses that were heavily populated prior to the EMP war.

The Explorer is not so concerned with mapping, although there is a market for that. Rather, s/he hunts the old technology, gasoline, and rare morsels of old world treats like candy-bars, and, of course, books. Books are extremely rare. What books were not destroyed by the nuclear blasts, the survivors burned for fuel or just out of hatred for how knowledge led to the destruction of the world. The Explorer keeps the books that

help him stay ahead of the game (and other Explorers). Other books, he'll sell to Inventors. After all, survival gear and travel means aren't cheap.

Occasionally, the Explorer will find a forbidden artifact from the Ancient world. While he knows these items are enhanced with what the Ancient world called magic, he might not know how to activate them. Some Explorers have succeeded, only to collapse near death as the artifact sucked out their life essence. In any case, such Ancient artifacts are real and highly sought after by those who know how to use them.

In fact, it might be the Explorer alone who knows that the Ancient Races still inhabit the world, though they are in hiding. No doubt he might cross paths with one or two of them, but he would never know it (since they use their magic to blend in with the Newborn Races). Well, the rest of the Steampunk era considers the Ancients as fully eradicated now, and besides, they're too busy with life's exciting Steam powered technological era to pay much attention to old races that died off.

But the Explorer knows better, and treads lightly. and although is perfectly capable of going it alone, the Explorer works well in groups, too, so long as no one tries to usurp his freedom. He knows he is the freest of all the vocations in the world.

All Explorers gain the following bonuses at character creation for free:

+1 PHL	Physical Trait +1: Fast
+1 COR	Physical Trait +1: Healthy
+1 WIL	Social Trait +1: Very Minor Inheritance I

They also receive bonuses based on ORank:

ORank	Boon
3	Physical Trait +3: Contortionist
5	Learning Trait +3: Trivia Genius
7*	Social Trait +3: Fixer Apprentice
10**	Social Trait +3/-3: Well-known / Secret Identity

* Explorers ignore the home region restriction in this trait; their Social Circles can be anywhere.

** If your actions as an Explorer have demanded that you had to survive by hiding under a Secret Identity, it should not be without some great gain your sacrifice has achieved, especially if you will suffer loss if your true self is ever exposed. It may be that you will never enjoy the praise of your legendary accomplishments, and can only hold your tongue when your Secret Identity gets all the credit (or blame).

If you like scavenging, looting and shooting, and discovering treasures others might kill for, this vocation might be a good pick for you. Odds are, you'll have minimum exposure to the politics of civilization, unless you stumble across something you really shouldn't have seen...

GAME PLAY

PART TWO

THE CORE THE CORE THE CORE

The core rules of Immortal Empires have not changed simply because we've moved forward in time. As you've seen up to this point, we still reference Traits and Flaws and character builds based in the Adventurer's Rulebook, and all systems that govern magic, poisons, game mechanics, etc., in that book and also the Storyteller's Codex are applicable to this rules expansion.

However, much of it needs to be updated for this age, especially the terminology of the world setting, and so we ask that you use this rules expansion as a lens through which to see the other rules, and help your Storyteller keep the Steampunk feel by understanding that some things in the AR and the SC just have to change while leaving the core mechanics in tact.

For instance, the monetary system surely has changed. Gold auraes and denarii are probably long lost, now replaced with a more modern paper currency of I.O.U.'s (commonly known as "notes" or "bank notes" which entitle the bearer to withdraw a pre-defined sum from a safe, secure place (called a bank). In less civilized areas of Steampunk, of course, bartering for goods or services will be the preferred commerce of the day.

Also, the social class structure may have changed, or at least the names of the classes (depending on how your Storyteller is telling things). In this expansion, Patricians have been replaced with "High Society." Equestrians and Plebeians are now "bourgeoisie" or "the poor" or more accurately, "those who do not hold High Society membership." While there surely will be slaves somewhere in some towns or regions, Steampunk society probably just calls them slaves, not "humiliorises."

So when you draw up your characters using the Adventurer's Rulebook, you'll have to do some on-the-spot interpretations and modifications, while leaving in tact the core rulebook's intended benefit or penalty. (If you have any doubts, be sure to ask the Storyteller to interpret/extrapolate it for you.)

Also, we might emphasize here that even in Steampunk, there are two overriding themes that should not be lost to the game: [1] everyone strives to become Emperor/Empress (it is, after all, how you can be said to "Win the game;" [2] there is still the ultimate war between the Presidium and the Nameless.

In the rest of this section, we will attempt to identify and Steampunk lens-correct certain aspects of both core rulebooks that may need more attention than changing a word or two.

GAME PLAY

While we certainly invite the Storyteller to extrapolate and write his or her own additional rules expansions for their own Steampunk story, we'll go ahead here and give some suggestions to try to keep everyone on the same page.

Synergy: A Modified Rule

It could well be that Talents (AR91-111) no longer have a place in a Steampunk world and are discarded completely by your Storyteller. This might be especially true in a world where magic users (i.e. Ancient and Starborn races) are hunted down and killed by the Newborn races (who do not have a great deal of Magical Affinity); Talents mimic magical effects, and even while not magical might get you killed.

Or it could simply be that the Storyteller wants a genuine Steampunk setting without the character enhancements and tweaks (minimalism) but loves this game system.

So here's an optional Rule modification concerning Synergy: Talents are no more! But Synergy still exists for another use which is yet to be discovered (as bodily battery-like power for cybernetic implants that become popular in the Cyber Age).

Also, we're here simplifying the calculation of Synergy: sum all of your Main Attribute Ranks and simply multiply that by 5 for your Max Synergy (instead of adding 8+7+6…etc.). Synergy Recovery is simply your Derived Attributes summed and

multiplied by 2 (and that's per hour). This seems reasonable to us, so that a maxed out Main Attributes section would yield 10x9x5 or 450 Synergy (Base) and 6x5x2 or 60 SGY Recovery per hour.

Remember, this is completely up to your Storyteller as to what type of story she is running. Perhaps you will be playing an Ancient Race character and you still have all your Talents (and Magic, but you'll have to use that sparingly). It's just that you'll have to make sure you don't use Talents in an overt way (at least when you're not solely among your fellow Ancients in your hidden settlement).

Or, it could be that you'll be playing a Newborn who is hunting a discovered Ancient Race outlaw, and the Storyteller wants to strip you of Talents to make you more reliant on Steampunk technology to take her down.

Both modes are acceptable and extremely fun.

Game Mechanics

The Creation Point, Experience and Fortune Point, Expertise Point system does not change. The d10 OPPROLL system is still in tact, complete with CRITs and CRITFAILs. REACTION and the Phase Combat system does not change.

If you are using the Cyber Age character records, there's a new Main Attribute: TAF (Technical Affinity) and some new Derived Attributes based on TAF. These have primary importance concerning BioTech enhancements attached to the body, and may, for Steampunk purposes, be non-applicable, especially if you're born in the middle of the Steampunk era, which is still quite a ways away from the Cyber Age. However, you'll have full use of them if you're a Time Traveler from the Future; just be aware that Steampunk societies will lust after your Tech or fear you (and thus want to kill you) if you display everything you've got in public.

There are some additional Game Mechanics we need in order to accommodate Steampunk weapons and armor, so we'll go over that in more detail in Combat & Tactics.

As for magic, it is still in the world, but the Magical Tapping Power replenishes at such a slow rate that the Ancients use magic only when extremely necessary. So, running across a magic caster, or even someone who has an *activated* magically enhanced item, would be very rare indeed. Same story for magical Fighting Arts, especially which cost MTAP per use.

Finally Social Standing is also redefined and recalculated.

Combat & Tactics

Since there is some new technology in this era, we have some additional weapon and armor terminology and rules we ask you to implement.

Let's start with ranged weapons: pistols, rifles, cannon, etc. First off, each ranged weapon has a Maximum Effective Range past which the damage its projectile causes much less damage.

Also, most projectiles in this era (and in Dead World, where we have more primitive black powder- accelerated projectiles), are able to pierce armor of different densities.

So, here's the new damage format for any weapon:

$$AP\text{-}nTx\text{-}MER$$

where AP is the Armor Piercing rating, n=Number of dice you get to roll, T simply means "Take", x=How many dice you get to take, and MER=Maximum Effective Range. That seen in a real example is:

Black Powder Flintlock Pistol W75: 10-7T3-100 with Armor Piercing .45 Caliber Rounds

which translates into: This black powder-propelled .45 caliber (approximate .45 inches) bullet from a rifled flintlock pistol (Workmanship of 75 means it fires normally 75% of the time, so 76%-100% is a misfire) would ignore up to 10DV (AP directly opposes DV), and you'd get to roll 7 dice and take 3 of those 7 as your damage (rerolling 10s), as long as the target you hit was within 100 Hexes of the pistol itself. Past the 100 yards, all numbers are decreased by 50% such that at 101 Hexes the projectile would have these stats: 5-3T1-50. Similarly at 151 Hexes, the projectile damage would be again decreased by 50% to 2-1T0-25 (utterly useless as it does no damage).

REMEMBER that we always round DOWN in this game. How often? ALWAYS.

We know that with impacts, the kinetic energy is changed to heat and a different vector of speed as the projectile ricochets. For those that penetrate, we will be ignoring this aspect completely, and by "penetration" we mean that the projectile has penetrated the DV (Defensive Value) to achieve at least ONE point of DAMAGE to the target (Body Value (BV)).

All material items have BV, living or not (a 2-ton ship might have 2000 BV, and this BV would be divided by its structural points something like Mast 1: 5%, Mast 2: 5%, Port Siding: 20%,

Starboard Siding: 20%, Deck: 20%, Hull: the rest. Likewise, each of those structural points might have different armor protections (or none at all) and thus their DV will vary.

This brings us to a Hard Core Rule: Ricochet. It is totally up to the Storyteller whether to implement the Rule as it will take another minute of game time, but we have tried to keep the rule simple enough for a game but accurate enough to satisfy those of you who want that added depth of realism.

RICOCHET

For impacts where the projectile does not penetrate the target, RICOCHET will happen, so long as the Storyteller judges the target to have substantially greater mass than the projectile, where knockback does not occur.

A ricochet flies off in a random direction to be determined by a d5: [1] up left, [2] up right, [3] left, [4] right, and [5] down.

A projectile only has half of its Maximum Effective Range, half its Armor Piercing rating, and half its Damage potential after it ricochets.

For those impacts (not necessarily projectiles) where it makes sense to have KNOCKBACK, remember that the advantage rests with the entity having the larger momentum (the AR allows knockback only if the "target is equal or lesser weight than you" (AR115) but that's for hand to hand combat).

Our special rule for KNOCKBACK for <u>high velocity</u> projectile (kinetic) impacts follows this formula:

DAMAGE RESISTED / 10 = # Hexes knockback

for the non-high-velocity target (that usually has the lower momentum). Remember to round down. If the weapon is NOT high velocity, this rules does not apply. Knockback will always follow the direction of the projectile's momentum. The Storyteller will have to do what makes sense (like if you got shot in the shoulder or leg as opposed to the torso). <u>Note that a projectile's AP (Armor Piercing rating), while opposed by DV, does NOT add to damage resisted for purposes of knockback, because it pierces armor instead of blunt force vs. armor.</u> (Unless specifically made to be armor piercing, most projectiles will have a ZERO or very low AP rating.) If High Velocity knockback does occur, the person knocked back should also suffer as many broken bones (each with 1 UFP) as Hexes knocked back.

Damage taken from secondary impact while being knocked back (say if you get knocked back into a brick wall) is equal to the number of Hexes you had left to be knocked back x d10s.

Range and Gravity

Although we're not going to elevate this to a Hardcore Rule, as it's best just ignored, the Storyteller can include physics that govern ballistics. The rules expansion for Cyber Age will cover this in more detail (for artillery projectiles and ICBMs), but here we'll just suggest this optional rule: Projectiles fall as many Hexes along the perpendicular to the gravitational plane as the gravity is strong, per second, absent any other consideration (like wind drag).

This falling (acceleration down) starts immediately (since gravity is always present), and subtracts from (if the projectile is going up) or adds to (if the projectile is going down) the projectile's vertical velocity, every second (for earth it would be 7.8 meters per second subtracted from/added to the projectile's vertical velocity each second (horizontal velocity would remain unaffected by this)).

So, the trick would be to assign a speed and an initial launch angle to know where the projectile would be in 1 second and extrapolate its path using a parabolic formula (there are standard equations for this, if you are that interested: see https://courses.lumenlearning.com/boundless-physics/chapter/projectile-motion/ (which explains it very well)).

SO, if the Storyteller wants to do all that, great, we leave it here as best untouched and just let Maximum Effective Range govern the roost!

Shielding and Weight

Especially in Steampunk, the best stuff weighs a lot, and it would be absurd for a puny little kid with PHQ0 to be able to walk around with heavy quarter-inch plates of steel for armor as if he were a PHQ5 grown man. Add to this nice steam inventions that necessitate carrying around heavy gallon-packs of water, hoses, your gear, weapons, and the like, to make yourself a one-man-arsenal.

Because of our Official Storyline, there will be some lightweight shielding (kevlar, etc.) that Explorers might scavenge and sell for a pricey price. In the Storyteller's Codex, we provided a hardness scale (SC118) by which Storytellers could make their own armor sets, but there were some complaints about this. Therefore, to the delight of our fans everywhere we've acquiesced and compiled a list or armor values.

In the table below, weight is averaged to 1 piece/plate of covering (arm/leg greaves, torso front, torso back, helmet, etc.), so that a full set of soft wood armor, for example, would be 4x arms (front & back), 4x legs, 2x torso, 1 helmet, each at 2 pounds for a total of 22 pounds of soft wood (dried out) armor.

nario; some armor is bulky, some make a lot of noise, some slow down certain body motions (or makes them impossible), and so on.

Unless materials mention thickness, all plates are assumed to be 1 inch thick (yes, we know in reality a lot of these plates are 0.26 to 1.7 inches thick, but we're simplifying it for a game). Modern Materials excluded (see Stacking Armor, below), doubling the thickness of Old World Materials increases the DV but also doubles the weight, and makes any scenario-based Storyteller penalty that much more severe (Storyteller, are you

BODY ARMOR VALUES

Old World Technique	Defensive Value (DV) vs.				Weight	Modern Tech	Defensive Value (DV) vs.				Weight
	Slash	Pierce	Blunt	HV	lbs/plate		Slash	Pierce	Blunt	HV	LBS
Padded/Stuffed Cloth	0	0	1	0	0	Nylon	7	7	5	0	5
Quilted/Embroidered Cloth	1	0	1	0	0	Hard Plastic	5	5	2	0	1
Soft Wood	1	1	2	0	2	Hard Rubber	8	3	20	0	2
Hard/Wet Wood	4	2	2	0	5	Plate (Titanium) 0.25"	50	50	50	40	200
Soft Leather	2	2	2	0	2	Plate (Tungsten) 0.25"	50	50	50**	50***	250
Hard Leather	3	4	5	0	3	Titanium Carbide 0.25"	75	75	75	55	225
Studded Leather	4	5	5	0	5	Tungsten Carbide 0.25"	100	100	100	65***	250
Light Chainmail (Steel)	5	5	4	0	7	Zylon (deteriorates fast)	10	8	12	10	3
Heavy Chainmail (Bronze)	6	5	5	0	9	Telephone Book	3	6	3	0	9
Scale (metal 0.25")	6	5	4	0	8	Graphite	25	5	25	25***	7
Shell (turtle/tortoise/clam)	5	7	2**	0	10	Aramid Fiber II (1" Kevlar)	7	7	7	25	1
Plate (Brass) 0.12"	7	7	7	0	7	Aramid Fiber III (2" Rimelig)	12	12	12	30	2
Plate (Iron) 0.12"	8	8	8	0	8	Polyethylene II (Spectra)	8	8	8	25	0.5
Plate (Bronze) 0.12"	9	9	9	1	7	Polyethylene III	15	15	15	30	1
Plate (Steel) 0.12"	10	10	10	2	8	Ceramic Plate (IV 1")	30	20	10	40***	10
Diamond	15	15	15	15***	10	Cyber Age MicroTech Suit	40	40	20	40	1
Skydrop Rock (Minerals)	20	20	20	20***	25	Cyber Age NanoTech Suit	50	50	30	50	0
Skydrop Steel	25	25	25	25	15	Cyber Age PicoTech Suit	50+	50+	50+	50+	0

Notes:

* Level I: Subsonic protection only; anti fragmentation & low velocity.

** 50/50 chance to shatter upon any blunt impact from a hard blow.

*** 80% chance to shatter upon HV impact

KEY: HV = High Velocity (Supersonic) Projectile

Example: Cyber Age NanoTech would include graphene, a nanomaterial (and single layer of graphite) that is 40 times stronger than diamond. The DV values given may or may not include slow penetration (like a very slow stab or scissors).

Because this system is piecemeal, you will be able to customize your armor how you see fit; even Cyber Age "suits" might be leggings only or torso only, while you have cool looking custom-designed arm greaves making you look badass. Cyber Age materials might not be available in your world (ST whim).

Other factors concerning each type of material will be for the Storyteller to add penalties/bonuses, depending on the sce-

listening?). So be wary of thinking that you're just going to have 10 plates of steel armor on every appendage thinking you're impervious...in fact, the knockback might just kill you!

Stacking Armor

So why are Modern Materials excluded from this? First, what we are really warning against is "stacking" plate upon plates.

Especially with High Velocity impacts, doubling plates for HV impacts is a bad idea, as the gap, no matter how slight, will actually cause the impact to inflict more kinetic damage; for game purposes, <u>this will mean that the Damage roll gets to TAKE ALL dice rolled (so a 7T3 HV projectile against stacked plates would turn into 7T7 damage!)</u>. At the same time, it should be acknowledged that combining different materials for Level I or slower attacks (arrows/H2H combat) might be beneficial.

Secondly, there comes a time when the efficacy of the material is "enough." Most modern armor is designed to protect you from ONE direct hit from a high velocity round, saving your life so you can get the heck out of there. Ceramic, graphite, graphene, and the like will all shatter upon impact, even while spreading out the force enough so that it won't cause damage to you. But without nanobots "fixing" the molecules (as in the case of a NanoTech suit), the next shot may well sink into your tender flesh!

Armor BV and Repairs

So when should repairs be needed for all armor then? For modern armor protecting against high velocity or some materials against blunt trauma, as soon as it shatters (see the asterisks?). For the rest, we suggest the following:

Armor Material	BV per Plate
non-metal Old World	50
Old World metal	100
Modern non-metal	80
Modern metal	200

This fits in nicely with the shield BV values we've already established (AR116), and keeps the armor useful for a while (since the defender is not going to sit there and let you keep hitting the same damaged part each time). Storytellers are, of course, welcome to develop their own special and unique BV lists.

Remember: Armor only takes BV damage for that which it successfully blocks from getting to your flesh. So the maximum BV damage an old world steel plate can take from any ONE hit (non-HV) is 10, with the rest of the rolled damage hurting your fragile self (if the damage was more than 10, that is). Armor piercing projectiles, while ignoring up to their AP rating in armor on their end, do exactly 1 BV of damage to armor per hit.

Remember, too, that the body armor values are representative of the entire worn plate, complete with seams and patches where the plates must be sewn or otherwise held onto the body; for this reason, the DV scale is not exactly representative of how many hundred times harder tungsten is than soft wood. For game simplification, our "linear" DV scale represents the exponential real-world concepts of hardness/tensile strength/shatter coefficient, etc., all in one.

Last Thoughts on Armor

Don't think you can just wear your amor all day, as you'll grow tired of all the extra weight and discomfort, and unfortunately incur Universal Fatigue Penalties (UFPs). Usually, the heavier and harder the armor, the faster the UFPs will pile up.

It takes a great deal of time to put armor on and take it off, even with help. Historically, it took a knight around 20 minutes to put on his full plate with his squire's help. Plan accordingly!

Finally, different materials are vulnerable (or resistant) to certain types of elemental attacks, and we'll leave that to the Storyteller's imagination (as even a soft, drift wood, highly flammable plate might be coated with a flame-retardant in her world), and who knows what she'll surprise you with when it comes to Cyber Age tech! BUT, we will mention that Ceramic Plate armor DOES directly oppose Armor Piercing rounds (the AP rating) on a 1 to 1 basis (but still has an 80% chance to shatter with each hit). *(Oh, and graphene superbly conducts electricity (but is this a vulnerability or does it make the armor deadly to approach?))*

Note: some modern armor deteriorates more quickly when exposed to the elements, especially moisture (c.f. Zylon). If you want to do your own research on this, here's a good place to start:

https://www.recoilweb.com/archives-body-armor-101-what-you-need-to-know-51103.html

We're also taking the liberty to suggest that you armor up your backpacks and vehicles, maybe even put some barding on your horse if you have one. The Immortal Empires Steampunk world isn't all just happy-go-lucky, you know.

Armor pieces: doublet, coif, hauberk, tabard, surcoat, pourpoint, gambeson, aketon, and plate armor pieces (cruisse, gaunlet, sabaton, besagew, bevor) can be made from the plate materials and do not add to the DV of the protected appendage, unless the piece is stacked under/over another armor (like a tabard of hard-embroidered cloth over plate or padded cloth under it).

For all armors and armor pieces, it's the Storyteller's job to assign limitations or penalties to Movement, Balance, Aware-

ness, etc., as is practical. Don't argue with the Storyteller about these things, just make note of it all, so you can call her out on it (nicely) if her badass Personalities aren't getting the same penalties.

And in case it went over your head: High Velocity (HV) means supersonic speed, but we're betting you're so smart you knew that already.

Dodging High Velocity Projectiles

Unless you have preternatural abilities, you will be unable to SK:Dodge high velocity projectiles (from handguns, rifles, cannon, etc.), and this is what makes them so dangerous!

POWERBASES

There are still the same types of Powerbases in our Steampunk setting as in the First through Seventh ages. But, we'll make some mention of them here so as to help everyone look at them through a Steampunk "lens."

Now everyone knows that there are basically six powerbases in Immortal Empires, all of which can be used to "become Emperor" (which is still the goal of this game!). These are the Socio-Economic (Popular), Political, Military, Magical, Foreign, and Criminal powerbases. In order to become Emperor/Empress of one of the five Ancient Races, you need(ed) to have three of these six powerbases at 1000 each but have a combined total score of 4000. Quite a challenge, that!

To become Mayor of a Steampunk town, however, you need only build a total (aggregate) score of 2000 with no one powerbase requiring any minimum.

The powerbase mechanism is a tool you and the Storyteller use to make sure you're not immediately accused of "treason" or some other high crime and misdemeanor and summarily executed by High Society zealots. If you've achieved the minimum score (2000), that means that you have some supporters in your town who (for good or for ill) recognize that you may have what it takes to be Mayor for longer than a day (and who will not be murdered in your sleep).

The Steampunk Lens

Having a military powerbase means you've got the Constable corps supporting you (at least those who hold any true persuasiveness, and who aren't afraid to take matters into their own hands to silence those who oppose you).

Your socio-economic powerbase in Steampunk goes hand-in-glove with your political powerbase, and represents how well you balance the demands of High Society with the admiration of the commonfolk (the masses). Catering too much to one will certainly piss off the other.

Having foreign powerful allies in other towns (other Mayors, Constables, High Society, criminals) who have an interest in your being the Mayor in your town also helps. And don't forget that being respected (and promising to reward) the criminal element in your town might be a worthy powerbase, too...

Finally, if you are able, enhance everything using your magical artifacts you've found. No one will be the wiser.

Magic & Aether

Part Three

Magic, though rare and highly guarded, can still be found in the Immortal Empires Steampunk era. Which types and how rare, are purely up to your Storyteller, but we'll include everything here, just in case your Storyteller includes everything, too.

As the old advanced science led directly to catastrophe of nuclear proportions, thinkers in the Steampunk era thirst for an alternate theory that explains the universe, and the concept of aether does that quite well. In the last half of this chapter, we'll explore how aether can be useful in the game, as our Official Storyline adopts its existence for Steampunk era through the Galactic Age.

For the First through Seventh Ages, aether is merely inconsequential as the high availability of magic made it obsolete (as with many other technological things that suddenly became desirable when magic became scarce; who needs a car when you can snap your fingers and Travel?).

Magic

Lesser and Greater Magic categorized by Schools (Alteration, Benediction, Curative, etc.) fall under the big umbrella called Refined Magic, and it makes an appearance from time to time in the Steampunk era, either as a rare artifact that survived the Cataclysm, or as direct evidence that there are still Ancient Races hiding in the shadows.

Because of the animus the Newborn races have against the Starborn (if any still exist, since they are likely not to have had the magical resources to survive Dead Age as did the Ancient Races), any open use of magic will immediately be punished by a death sentence and summarily executed. Hence, magic use is, for the most part, only done in secret, especially since casting with the magic being invisible to the naked eye/no hands cast can be quite expensive (AR131).

Likewise, magical fighting art powers are rarely used without the assurance that the opponent will not live to speak of it, since many of them are clearly hallmarks of preternatural ability (even subtle things like the eyes changing completely black is a big no-no in modern society!).

Because MTAP replenishes at such a slow rate (Dead World was 1d5 or 1d10 per year, Storyteller Whim), the surviving Ancient Races are likely to have reserved its use to massive (and long-lasting) shapeshifting spells so they can appear to be any one of the Newborn races among whom they live. Artifacts and MenH items that achieve this goal, as well, would be highly coveted.

Original (Unrefined) Magic

Keeping to the same out-of-sight, out-of-mind practices as Lesser/Greater magic use, at least until technology advances to where certain magical effects can be explained away by it (or, if there are still Talents in the world, by them), Original Magic may or may not still be in your world, depending on your Storyteller's story.

What's certain about it, though, is that if it is, it will be even more scarce and highly guarded than Refined Magic, as it is much more deadly, being merely the raw magical power of a person's Willpower touching the Weave to achieve whatever that person's imagination has conjured up, and let's not forget the supremely dangerous Circles of Ten (or, worse yet, Circles of One Hundred, if some immortals get together).

It is possible, though, that eventually, some things, like Starfire, might be able to be explained away through some technological device (like a powerful laser).

If Original Magic is not lost to your world, the smart Ancient Races will have foreseen a need for it and will have several thousand MenH items bathed in Energy Baths for centuries (because of Dead World, items would gain 1 point of Binding per year (not one per week)).

The big caveat here is that the Overmind, which consists of powerful Ancient Races who were centering on leyline plexuses during the EMP cataclysm, may also know about Original Magic...are you beginning to see how dangerous the Overmind really is?

For the Steampunk era, the big thrill is really finding a magical artifact in some forgotten cave somewhere that still is in an energy bath. It might have hundreds of Binding, which depletes at a rate of 1 Binding point per day out of the bath. But if you're lucky enough to find such an item and figure out how to use it, you may just tip the scales in your favor for a while, at least until the word gets around that you're an Ancient race impostor using magic and need to be executed.

Let's just say here, too, that it is entirely possible that some of the Ancient Races who have been Shapeshifted for so long might actually have gone mad. And what about all the vampires and other monsters not dependent on the connection to the Illumination or Fey Realm Dimensions? Well, that's up to your

Storyteller. If you're playing True Steampunk, the monsters will be the result of failed experiments, not something arising from the Shadowscape. Remember that Steampunk era folks could label you a "monster" just for being an Ancient Race.

This is where your reputation is extremely important. You can find and use publicly all the MenH items you can, so long as no one starts thinking you're really an Arkadian, Astorian, Ammorian, Oshekogan, or Atlantean, and those who are whispering in the shadows that you are should meet with a swift and deadly "accident."

OFF GRID, of course, you might be able to survive a reputation as the "Ammorian Assassin," for example, and it might even enhance the awe others have of you Off Grid. That will be your call, even if you aren't truly an Ammorian. What matters Off Grid is that you keep your word, do what you said you would do, and stay alive.

Avatar & Celestial Magic

Avatar-level magic might also be in your world, and it is just as powerful as ever (but also just as costly), so don't think that every Ancient Race is some punk cowering behind a tree somewhere.

Ancient Race Avatars will still guide their races, even in hiding, since their purpose is to protect them from the wiles of the Marunes (oh yes, my friend, the Marunes are still in the Steampunk world, too, though their machinations are much more hidden and manipulative behind the scenes). Avatars must ensure their race, and ultimately, their immortal heroes survive unto the time the Presidium returns for their Star Legions.

Powerful Celestial Magic might also appear from time to time in the Steampunk era, as Time Travelers from the future might bring their picotech-Greater/Original Magic enhanced artifacts with them (remember the weird hand-glovey thing the alien "Ra" wore in the movie *Stargate*? That alone made him appear Power-like (not to mention his ability to body-hop and his big-ass spaceship). Of course, we all know that the glovey thing was merely a device that had radio-active pico-particles interacting with his Willpower (and the subsequent Original Magic) to create a deadly wave of gamma radiation that killed whomever he aimed it at.

You can, of course, find other examples of Celestial Magic in other tales of the future or distant past (a light saber, perhaps; a beam-me-up-Scotty transport; maybe even a cold fusion reactor that magic ensures remains stable; and maybe even the Star-

gate itself). Celestial Magic items in your world should be no less awesome than these examples, but the odds of your finding one are probably slim to none.

In any case, the bottom line is that magic, in any form, is very rare, and if you find it, you'd be wise to hide it again, at least until you're sure you can use it without suffering one of its many risks.

Aether

Since aether has been abandoned by our own world's scientific community in favor of relativity, it can be a hard concept to wrap one's head around. But we'll make an attempt here so that you may be able to benefit from its in-game existence.

AETHER ISOLATION MACHINE

EVERY CONSTABLE SHOULD HAVE ONE

First off, for the Immortal Empires Official Storyline, we'll be adopting aether and aether-based physics, since it fits in so nicely with our magical ecosystem (and because we *want* to hear things go "boom" in space!). In our game world, the "vacuum" of space isn't empty; it's filled with luminiferous aether, which serves as a substratum through which waves like light and sound can propagate. But we're also able to make true vacuums by sucking out everything (even aether) from a sealed container, so sound can't travel.

That said, one of the most basic rules of aether-based physics is aether-created gravity, which is caused by a vortex (created by something spinning) of aether, which produces a low pressure area to which higher pressure areas naturally move towards.

In this way, the spinning earth creates its low pressure vortex in space, which produces the low pressure area, which causes the moon to move towards the earth, at least until the pressures reach equilibrium (at which point they'll stop moving towards each other) or until, as in the moon's case, their velocity around the vortex has kept it from falling further into the vortex.

With just this one aspect of aether theory we can think of several fantastic uses: graviton beams, slingshot space travel (focusing extremely fast-spinning aether funnel at huge high pressure space), hand-held disarming devices or devices that pull an object (or person) towards you, and so on.

So, if we're using aether theory, does that mean that other scientific stuff is left out? Well, we'll have to get rid of Special Relativity in favor of Clock Retardation thusly: Contrary to special relativity, movement doesn't affect time; rather, the motion through aether causes a slowing down of moving clocks. Thus, deep space travel may be more easily achieved through aether (as well as Time Travel, if one can "move" fast enough through the aether to make the clock actually go backwards.

Otherwise, we see no reason why we can't just add aether to existence (it might even be the "dark matter" that our science says fills much more space (25%) than baryonic matter (5%). Scientists also say there's a "dark energy" which repels gravity (70%), which could easily be aether itself (since aether physics demands that equal pressure areas would repel each other). It also could explain the actual phenomenon known as gravitational lensing.

For more information on dark matter, feel free to read the same article we read at:

https://www.nationalgeographic.com/science/space/dark-matter/

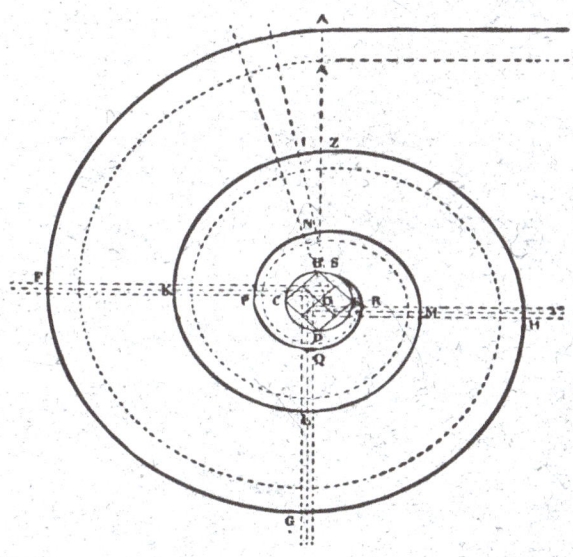

Ok, we're not here trying to do a treatise on aether theory, so that's enough on the technical stuff, but we wanted to say something about it so that you can have some foundation for "logically" using it in the game.

So it seems like aether is great for the Galactic Age, but how does any of it apply to the Steampunk Era? Well, we've got a few ideas about that.

True steampunk will have it so that aether does not exist lower than the heavens, and so anyone trying to sell you an aether isolation machine is probably a charlatan. Of course, discussion of aether might find its way into High Society dinner party debates, but otherwise, it's merely a theory, for now.

On the other hand, perhaps your Storyteller has allowed a little aether to seep into the air of your world and with the help of a little magic, perhaps, someone might be able to make a machine that separates it (even though you can't see it — it's like dark matter), and allows it to be used to boost certain weapons/devices with power (dark energy).

In case your Storyteller is running the second scenario, we've included below a list of cool aether-enhanced (AenH) items. While the abbreviation looks familiar to magically-enhanced (MenH), the number after that abbreviation represents not a "binding" but how many uses of aether has left of its maximum aether volume:

AenH-4/10 Pistol W99: 7T5/7T3

This would mean the pistol has 4 aether "boosts" left of its 10 capacity, where the damage from the projectile would be 7T5,

and once the aether is depleted, the damage would revert to a "normal" non-AenH damage of 7T3, and the pistol currently has a Workmanship rating of 99%.

Obviously, what we're doing here is using aether like modern-day Nitro. And that's okay. So, used properly, aether (anti-matter that has "boosting" capabilities like nitro), can have many applications.

But the workmanship for any AenH item or construct can never fall below 96% without the thing becoming unstable and possibly exploding or disintegrating with dire effects to anything within a certain radius (which the Storyteller knows). But suffice it here to say that the greater amount of contained aether, the larger the radius of effect will be (and more powerful the explosion/disintegration). Damage sustained to the aether-related workings of the item will lower the Workmanship rating, so it would be wise to shield and protect *these parts* with great care.

If not a weapon, but say an AenH skyship, the shorthand would probably look something like:

AenH-3/3 Johnson Skyship Mk1 W99: 100/50 Hx/Ph

This would mean that the Johnson Mark 1 Skyship is Aether-Enhanced with 3 bursts of 3 available, and each burst grants 100 Hexes/Phase movement instead of its normal 50. In this case, the burst lasts for only 1 Phase, but you can easily add how many Phases each burst will last, if you have such a great and awesome Skyship (perhaps Mk 2 or 3!).

For some AenH items, there might be other limitations on their use, which may be out of necessity lest the item overheat or destroy itself if used too often in too short a time, and the like. But all of that would be imposed by the Inventor and hopefully passed on in the directions with the item (otherwise, you might be taking an awful chance if you decide to use one of these items without knowing the manufacturer's warnings...).

SHIELDING & WEAPONRY

PART FOUR

Although we've already touched on armor and weaponry in the Part 2 (page 24), we revisit all of it here to provide some deeper context and to expand on it with some interesting Steamtech ideas.

When we say Dead World, we're talking about what Steampunkers would call the "Old World," or the world that existed before the nuke-blasts. That world was very advanced in technology (duh! It had nukes...), but we mean that some of that tech (though very little) will have survived to what we here call "Modern Day," i.e., the Steampunk Era.

So, we'll use Dead World/Old World armor and weaponry as a baseline for what could be available in our modern Steampunk era. We've also included some additional shielding and weapons not mentioned earlier.

Modern Armor

Nylon is Dead World tech that has made it through the ages due to its long shelf life. It doesn't have High Velocity (HV) protection, but can be used to counter small Steampunk era arms and slashing weapons. Slash-proof nylon is a special weave that adds DV5 against Slashing and Piercing attacks.

Spider web silk is several times stronger than steel, and has the bullet-catching properties of Aramid Fiber, with 3-times the strength and 25-times the elasticity. This means that it can be made into comfortable clothing that can be worn every day.

In the Steampunk world, this is the everyday armor of the High Society man or woman who can afford the full body "underwear" from one's neck all the way down to the bottom of the feet. It's strong enough and durable enough to be made into any type of clothing one can think of (including ski-masks, for those Explorers who need to survive lurking bandits!). It's just expensive and requires a very patient and skilled weaver and spider-farm to get.

Clothing Type & DV	Slash	Pierce	Blunt	HV	Weight
Arakhne fiber shirt	3	3	0	15	1
Arakhne fiber pants	3	3	0	15	1
Arakhne fiber overcoat	4	4	1	20	3
Arakhne fiber underwear	2	2	0	5	2

Plate armor is Dead World tech and is mechanical armor which utilizes servos powered by electric or EV motors with dry cell rechargeable batteries. They are very heavy as full suits, but might be usable in Steampunk as single pieces for torso front or back, etc.

They are usually found without any electric motors or batteries still intact and thus must be retrofitted in order to be used as complete suits. Ideally, the complete mechanized suit is air tight, complete with its own oxygen mix and cooling or heating system. But in Steampunk, the rubber for the air tight fittings has usually been rotted out but that's not to say they cannot be resealed somehow.

Some armor might be found in protected military forts, shells that for some reason or other survived the nuke war, and will have a power supply that can be recharged using steam generators. To accomplish the recharging, enough generators have to be crossed over for a 105 amp through-put. A typical generator at 25 turns per second will create 20 amps. That means a steam engine will have to operate at 1500 rmps and turn 6 generators to charge the suits. This will take 4 to 6 hours to charge, depending on the quality of the battery. A 4-hour charge will last for 2 hours, and a 6-hour charge will last for 3 hours, regardless as to whether the suit is being used or otherwise "turned on."

It is possible that some prototypes of mechanical armor could use hydraulic power instead of electric. Good luck finding the fluid!

Zylon is hardly worth mentioning, being a Dead World tech that probably has not survived to this day, as it deteriorates quickly when exposed to light and heat.

Aramid Fiber is the cheapest and most readily found Dead World armor tech. It is typically military grade and therefore camouflaged. The discovery of Spider web silk has made the re-fabrication of Aramid Fiber obsolete but it is still a good haul if one can find it. Usually, Aramid fiber vests and jackets and leg coverings will have tungsten carbide disks sewed inside of the material, increasing some protections.

Availability of these armor types will depend greatly on your Storyteller's whim...

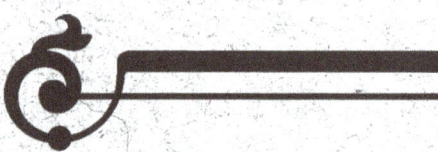

Modern Weaponry

As we already know from the Adventurer's Rulebook, all weapons have a weapon Rank. If you do not have your skill ranked up to the minimum weapon rank, you'll still be able to use the weapon (so long as figuring out how to pull the trigger is intuitive enough), but you will suffer the [P]enalty die while doing so (and you won't be able to make any called shots or have any aiming worth shit).

If the weapon has an armor piercing (AP) rating, remember that this directly opposes a target's DV before any damage is rolled. If DV is fully depleted, AP rating points does NOT overflow to be added to damage. If, however, some DV still remains after the AP has been applied to it, damage must overcome the remaining DV first before it can be applied to the BV of a person or target object.

Only Dead World ammunitions have AP qualities, normally, as Steampunk munitions have yet to re-invent the hardening or chemicals that allow a High Velocity projectile to ignore armor.

Primitive ranged weapons are big and bulky and usually frowned upon when walking through even the smallest villages. But the use of them for hunting or self-protection has become very popular due to their ease of manufacturing and the ability to produce new ammunition without the need for large production plants. These include the short bow, long bow, recurve bow, compound bow, pocket crossbow, and the crossbow.

These weapon stats are listed below; remember arrows are Piercing weapons:

Weapon Rank	Weapon	Speed (PhAct)	Damage/MER (Hexes)
1	Short bow	1/3	1T1 - 30
2	Long Bow	1/2	3T1+5 - 50
3	Recurve Bow	1/2	5T3+PHQ - 80
4	Compound bow	1/2	1T1 per 10lbs pull (Max 60lbs)
1	Pocket Crossbow	1	1T1x2 - 10
1 per 50 lbs pull	Crossbow	1	1T1x2 per 50 lbs draw (max 250 lbs)

Shotguns come in many different sizes. Dead World slugs have an AP10. Buckshot does not have AP qualities. All pump or semi-automatic shotguns have a PhAct of 1/3. Single shot or double barrel shotguns have that many shots per round, but will otherwise have a PhAct of 1 to take into account the reload factor.

Weapon Rank	Weapon	Type	Workmanship/Damage/MER (Hexes)
1	20 gauge (buck)	P	W98-3T3-30
2	20 gauge (slug)	HV	W98-4T3-50
1	12 gauge (buck)	P	W98-4T4-30
2	12 gauge (slug)	HV	W98-5T4-50
3	10 gauge (buck)	P	W98-5T5-30
3	10 gauge (slug)	HV	W98-6T5-50
4	8 gauge (buck)	P	W98-6T6-30
4	8 gauge (slug)	HV	W98-7T7-50

The Storyteller should also take into account buckshot spread (a cone) to one hex diameter at Max Effective Range (MER).

Rifles have barrels which have been rifled for accuracy. Dead World rifles have AP10 for small (.177 to .270), AP15 for medium (.30 to .375), and AP25 for large (.376 to .50) calibers. Each rifle can be effectively fired 3 times every PhAct. Faster fires will incur the penalty die and preclude aiming.

Weapon Rank	Weapon	Type	Workmanship/Damage/MER (Hexes)
1	Small hunting	HV	W98-3T2-150
3	Medium hunting	HV	W98-4T3-200
5	Large hunting	HV	W98-5T4-400

Assault rifles are all Dead World tech. They share the same calibers as rifles, but are infinitely more valuable due to their high capacity ammunition magazines and cyclic firing rate.

The problem with these great Dead World weapons, is, of course, ammunition, or more specifically, the refined smokeless black powder that is no longer readily available in the Steampunk era, and if it is, it might be playing host to some radio active fallout. But if you can get those somehow, all the more power....

Machine guns are less accurate than any rifle. Small machine guns use medium size pistol ammunitions and have an AP10. Medium caliber Machine guns use small caliber rifle ammunition. Large caliber machine guns use medium caliber ammunition.

Important: You should NOT use Steampunk era ammunition in Dead/Old World machine guns; if you do, they might jam on you, at least until Steampunk inventors re-discover how to refine black powder to the standard it was before (and then put it in nicely sealed compact bullets, and *then* chain them all together for the quick action machine guns are capable of.

Dead World *pistols* all have an AP rating, but this varies based on caliber: Small calibers (.22 to .32) have an AP5; Medium calibers (.357 to .40) have an AP10; Large calibers (.41 to .50) have an AP15. Steampunk munitions have the same damage and MER (max eff. range), but lack the AP qualities of the Dead World munitions. They all can produce High Velocity (HV) impacts.

Weapon Rank	Weapon	PhAct	Workmanship/Damage/MER (Hexes)
2	Revolver, Small	1/6	W98-6T2-30
3	Revolver, Medium	1/3	W98-7T3-50
4	Revolver, Large	1/2	W98-7T5-75
2	Semi-auto, Small	1/10	W98-5T2-30
3	Semi-auto, Med	1/6	W98-7T3-50
4	Semi-auto, Large	1/3	W98-7T5-75

Semi-automatic pistols can only use Dead World munitions. Their caliber and AP rating are the same as their revolver counterparts, but they have a greater firing speed.

Air, or pneumatic, rifles have become viable weapons due to the advancement in speed and accuracy. For an air rifle to be useful for self-promotion or hunting it has to exceed 1000 feet per second (ft/s). These air rifles below are representative of those air rifles and range from 1000 to 1500 ft/s. All air rifles are silent and none of them have AP qualities. They are short range weapons, but have the advantage of only needing a projectile and an air-pump to use them.

Air tanks come in three sizes: 1500 psi tanks are good for 6 shots; 3000 psi tanks are good for 12 shots; 4500 psi tanks are good for 18 shots. Due to size restraints, no tanks larger than

4500 psi can be attached to an air rifle. Simple bicycle-stule pumps can be purchased to the psi specification and take 3 minutes to fill the air tanks. Pneumatically powered projectiles are still considered High Velocity projectiles (unable to be Dodged without preternatural ability), and they can be fired 3 times per phase (PhAct = 1/3).

Weapon Rank	Weapon	Workmanship/Damage/MER (Hexes)
1	Pneumatic Rifle, Small	W98-1T1-10
3	Pneumatic Rifle, Medium	W98-2T2-30
5	Pneumatic Rifle, Large	W98-4T3-50

Heavy Weapons

The steam, or pneumatic, cannon is Steampunk tech that rivals its Dead World counterpart. Pneumatic cannon that use shot have no AP value, but hit everything in a 10 hex radius if the target is at least 50 hexes away. One shot per phase.

Weapon Rank	Weapon	Workmanship/Damage/MER (Hexes)
5	Steam cannon (5 lbs)	W98-5T3x10-520
5	Steam cannon (10 lbs)	W98-8T6x10-420
5	Steam cannon (20 lbs)	W98-10T8x10-300
5	Steam cannon (20 lb shot)	W98-10T8x10-300

Then there are **Dead World cannon** that, if found, ould change the face of battle completely. They are powerful and can easily take down any armored vehicle from this era or the past. Each of these can fire one shell each Phase and have armor piercing:

Weapon Rank	Weapon	Workmanship/Damage/MER (Hexes)
5	Cannon 5"	W98-50-10T8x10-2000
5	Cannon 10" 2 man team	W98-100-10T9x10-3500
5	Cannon 16" 3 man team	W98-200-10T10x10-7000

There's more out there, but this should get your mouth watering. Keep in mind, if a nuke is found, the possibility of getting it to work is basically nonexistent. How-to manuals just don't exist, and serious monkeying with it could be slightly dangerous.

THE NITTY GRITTY

Practical Observations from one of our Contributers, T. Helvey

During the nuclear apocalypse most of the oil wells and oil-supplying countries were targeted. Thus, petroleum is one of the rarest commodities on the market. While there are small pockets found here and there, the amount is not enough to start a progressive move towards combustion engines, and if one were to find one, they would soon find themselves on the short list of many organizations that wish to steal it...at any cost!

At some point in the Steampunk era, steam power will have brought stability to the world. Steam is a resource that can be had by anyone, and its regulations is impossible. Small magnetic brush electric generators make it viable for even the most remote home in the country to have power readily available, so long as they have burnable material.

A steam engine is generally an easy machine to build. You need a tank for water to be heated (boiler), a sealed cylinder for a piston to go up and down (or side to side), a crank shaft to direct the energy, and a flywheel to transfer the energy to the desired location (or a turbine to generate the electricity).

There are batteries in this era, but the Dead World (pre-Nuke) batteries are few and far in between and Steampunk era batteries are rudimentary, at best. They are mainly alkaline, which are inherently hard to charge. The flooded lead cell batteries of old can be copied, but without the petroleum to build the stable plastic cases, they are huge and cumbersome and cannot be used in vehicles to make electric vehicles (EVs). They need huge production plants and a stable government to support their production, so they are rare. The alkaline batteries are extremely unwieldy by they are easy to make and having one in a home or many in a factory makes their bulk somewhat more acceptable, but using one to power a vehicle is near impossible (unless you haul it on a trailer).

This does not mean that Steampunk era builders cannot use electric motors to power their steam vehicles. In fact, the most efficient form of vehicle power has been electric motors powered by steam engine generators. The generator is mounted in the trunk of the car and the engine can be attached to a transmission or attached to an axle for propulsion. The steam engine's relatively low flywheel speed means that it needs to be geared correctly, however, to get to the speeds that are required.

LEGACY TECH RETROFITTING. Whether it's a train or an automobile, every legacy tech vehicle can be retrofitted to be able to run on steam. The only exceptions are jets and large aircraft, where steam and generators can never achieve the power levels required. Small planes have been created, presumably, but even retrofitting small aircraft can shorten your life, as it might well take you longer than expected. When taking to the air, these days, you merely need a good dirigible, or "dig," as I call them.

There are three types of motors in this era: permanent magnet motors (PMDC), field energized motors, and steam motors. PMDC motors are small and lightweight, which makes them ideal for smaller vehicles or machines, to include bikes and carriages, but they lack in power and durability. For larger vehicles, field energized motors are used. This type consists of an electromagnetic brush motor, much the same as the PMDC, only the magnetic charge is provided by a power circuit. Here's a chart to simplify things:

Type of Vehicle	Voltage	Amps
Two wheeled	24-48	50
Carriage	48-72	400
Small Car	72-108	400
Average Car	120-150	500
Delivery Van	155-200	600-1000
Semi-truck/Train (Engine only)	300+	1000+

A general size guideline for finding the size of a generator is that a 50-amp generator is roughly 5 inches wide and 15 inches long. It weighs roughly 20 lbs. So if you were to need 500 amps, you would need ten times that (but only multiply the width and weight): 50 inches wide by 15 inches high and it would weigh 200 lbs. This would be driven by a steam engine that would weigh another 200 lbs without fuel and water, both of which (at roughly 8 lbs/gallon) would add another couple hundred pounds.

You can see where weight can get out of hand pretty quickly and vehicles can become large and very interesting looking. With the main building component being copper due to its relative easy of smelting, forming and conductivity, this means that there are some pretty shiny vehicles driving around, some clunkers, some quieter, but all with lots and lots of steam!

These amperes are also indicative of a vehicle that will be traveling at under 40mph. To increase the speed of these vehicles, to double the speed to 80mph, you would multiply the amperes by 8 for 4000 amps.. Using equal divisions, to go to 50mph in an average car you would need 1000 amps, to go to 60mph you would need 2000 amps, to go to 70mph, 3000 amps. You can get the same effect by using gears found in a transmission. A 1-to-1 ratio is usually found in one of those gears, third gear in most, and after that increases in gear size will create greater speed. Carriages and those vehicles that do not use gears will find that transference will be 1:1 to the axle.

Steamtech Game Mechanics

Part Five

So how do we implement all this new technology into the game system in order to maintain a balanced and fair system? Without some type of game system for it, you're likely to come up with some type of machine that rouses the ire of your Storyteller because it's able to level a town at the press of a button.

Well, we argue that's nothing new in Immortal Empires! We've long had some Lesser Magic that was capable of destroying a town, let alone Greater and Avatar-level magic. But there's a slight change, starting with the Dead Age: the Magitarii and Frumentarii just don't have enough magical resources any longer to show up within seconds of your breaking the law in order to haul you off in First Age manacles and put you in The Chair for trial. So, that tool the Storyteller had to keep you in check is now lacking.

We're not saying that something won't show up to smack you down to size (there will be plenty of Immortals around, as well as Cabal and Marune Minions), but they'd have to think it was worth the expenditure of their precious MTAP to make you answer for something egregious.

As for mundane law enforcement, there just might not be enough Constables (and they might not have enough "hero" power, being Normals (ORank Zero)) to keep you in check.

And if we know Gamers, we know you're going to try to push the game to the limits until the Storyteller admits defeat!

So, you gave us no choice but to implement a system to make you earn the glory you seek, to ensure your rise to power can't happen over night. But, don't look at it as trying to keep you down! The same system is applied to your enemies, too, so that peasant Cog you've slapped around can't just wake up the next day with some powerful machine, press a button, and have you disintegrated.

Hmmmm. I wonder if aether will be able to do that....

Anyway, we digress. the system is in place to protect you as well, is what we mean to say. And while you're reading about it, please forget that in this Age it's going to be much harder to investigate and punish any crimes you might commit. We wouldn't want to encourage Off Grid ambitions.

Besides, the Storyteller just might have a relative of Van Helsing introduce Forensics a little early in your town...

Reliability, Instability, and Power

We've already introduced Reliability under the concept of Workmanship. The Workmanship Rating is a percentage that something will function as it is meant to. Hence, a W75 would mean that there is a 75% chance for the item/machine to function normally, and that any roll of 76% to 100% means the item fails in some way (with 00 meaning a CRITFAIL, such that the item fails in some BIG way).

All mechanical devices that are not simple machines (lever, wheel and axle, pulley, inclined plane, wedge, and screw) is subject to the Storyteller's assignment of a Workmanship (Reliability) rating. And if the simple machine is so old as to be deteriorating (a rusty screw or rotting inclined wooden plane), then those get assigned one as well. After all, hardly anything is made of Dream Essence anymore...

For Workmanship purposes, those who are hand-crafting an item using their own skills receive a base Workmanship depending on their Rank in that skill: W Base 10 for Rank 1, W Base 20 for Rank 2, 30 for Rank 3, 40 for Rank 4, and 50 for Rank 5. Thus, a R5 Weaponsmith need only roll a 50 to max Workmanship out at 99% (which is the highest Workmanship without venturing into the magical/artifact arena).

Factories and machine-made items will have a Workmanship rating that ultimately depends on who put the factory together, as an average of those skills used (and the people who built the factory machines).

Instability

Stability depends on the number of moving parts or programmable components and can be thought of as a converse to Reliability. The more moving parts or programmed components, the more Instability is likely to occur.

Thus, instability starts at zero with no moving parts, and gradually increases one by one with each addition. The resulting aggregate number is the percentage that Instability will happen and one of those parts (or programmable components) will become unstable and either break or fail to function properly.

Let's take, for example, a Steam-powered Dirigible with two huge propellers, two large steam pipes attached to the balloon, and one huge rudder. That's five main components for 5% chance that something of the Dirigible might stop working correctly. Even though it has a Workmanship Rating of 95%, and that check is easily made, the moving parts might start wobbling because of some type of manufacturer error during installation. The propellers are completely intact and reliable, but the header they're seated on might be moving about.

But hold on just a minute. While Workmanship is checked as often as the Storyteller desires, Instability isn't as annoying, and might never come in to play. That's because in order for something to become unstable, it has to have sustained at least one point of damage to its component system. Without any damage it is ASSUMED that the machine had everything installed correctly and will function normally (Inventors take pride in their reputation, after all).

So if your dirigible starts wobbling apart on its maiden flight, you'd better start looking for a saboteur (which could be the Inventor, of course), because the Game System is not just going to "stick it to you" like that.

Only one Instability check is made for any damage incident, and that one check for the entire system (we wouldn't have to roll 5 times: each propeller, each steam pipe, and the rudder).

Should your machine sustain damage again, another Instability check would be made at that time for the whole system.

Unstable Positive Result

If something shows up as unstable, it doesn't mean that the instability makes the machine cease functioning right away. Your Storyteller knows exactly how long before the thing falls apart if you keep operating it while it is unstable, and perhaps with an appropriate attribute or skill roll, you'll know, too.

It might be best to shut the machine down before it falls apart, in order to save wobbly but completely reliable components from becoming unreliable (or broken).

Component Targeting and Shielding

If your airship, say, is being targeted by an enemy that calls specific areas to hit, like your rudder, then they must suffer a [P]enalty die to their Attack roll. If their attack misses the called shot but is still high enough to hit your airship without the called shot, it will still be a successful hit (but to a random part of the ship, with the called shot item not possible among the randoms).

Depending on the material your components are made of, they will have a higher or lower BV (Body Value). That is why it is good to place shielding around your vulnerable components.

Shielding in this sense is not DV (Defensive Value), which is, in essence Damage Reduction. Instead, shielding would be some other type of material that also has BV that must be widdled away to zero before your vulnerable component can be damaged.

While all this sounds fine and dandy and like, well, duh! Of course I'd shield the components... Just remember that shielding is an extra cost for your machine (which already might be very costly) and it has practical implications, such as being HEAVY, so it might not be the best thing to add to your airship, for instance, if your airship can't get off the ground!

Intentional Instability (Sabotage)

Done right, Instability adds an exciting dimension to the game; it might be that you'll want to sabotage an enemy's machine, and will delight when it wobbles apart while he is strutting his pride in front of the Mayor and the rest of High Society! For that, we've added some bonuses to Intentional Instability. There are a variety of skills out there you can use for sabotage, and the Storyteller will know which of them applies best to any situation, but our baseline is this: You get 100% of your sabotage skill role towards the Instability percentage of a machine so long as the skill you're using is directly related to the science of the component you're sabotaging.

So, say you're going to sabotage an electric grid and you roll a whopping TN35. If you have SK:Electrical Engineering, that's directly related, and you get +35% to its base Instability. Also, Intentional Instability (sabotage) is cumulative with other sabotage (if you or someone else has sabotaged other components).

If, however, the skill is not directly related, then the Storyteller will assign a fraction commensurate with how related it is, such that you might not get your full roll towards the sabotage.

Power

Steampunk machines are notoriously inefficient. Much energy (power) is lost to leaky pipes, heat, and other factors such as sprawling tubular networks that allow cooling from compartment to compartment.

This is especially true when it comes to bigger machines that pump out more power. More power means more energy escaping in more ways. While not getting into the nitty gritty

of a diminishing return graph which would show a curve that plateaus at a certain point (see below):

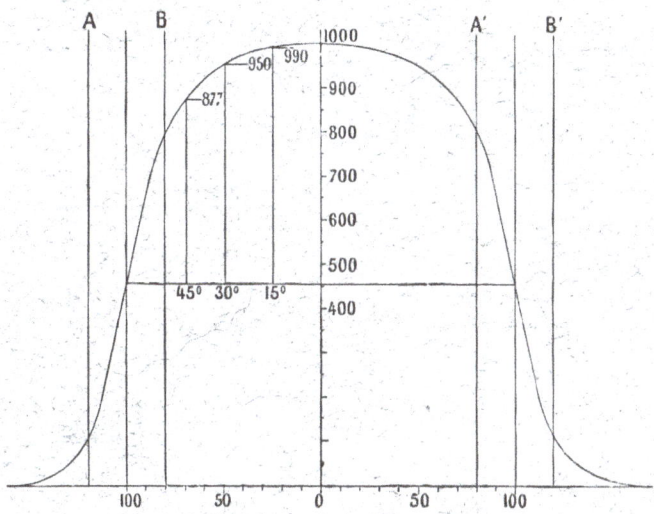

there is a perfect balance of power input to power output, which is ideal for a particular machine. If not enough energy (the left side of the graph), the output power is lower. If too much energy (the right side), the output power starts to diminish as well because the machine just cannot harness it all.

At least this will be true for the Steampunk era (we know that as machines become more efficient, this graph will have a wider and higher plateau with a much quicker falloff on either side).

This brings our semi-technical discussion to the interesting subject of a Steam Turbine Science. If the turbine does not have the correct settings: inlet mass flow equaling outlet mass flow, the correct pressure, the correct temperature, then the turbine will suffer condensation and the electricity output will be diminished.

We say all that to say this: the Storyteller will rightly assign difficulty tasks to Players who want to invent great things, depending on the complexity of the machine and the power that the machine needs to consume in order to function. The greater the power your machine delivers (say, to level a town), the more overwhelming will be the power consumption and in-game requirements the Storyteller should place on you.

Even in our own world and age, tech giants position their factories near dams because they need more and more power as their computer chips get smaller and smaller (to be technical, the electrons more easily tunnel through a gate dialectric that is only a few atomic layers (10-11 angstroms) wide, thus causing much leakage); thus the current is leaking as much power as it is using. Real world example: a tech/search engine company placing their headquarters near the a huge dam; if they're using 50,000-100,000 processors, they could easily be consuming ten megawatts of power (at an average cost of about $60,000 every 24 hours if they had to buy it from the electric company!).

So, we'll take a step back from getting so technical (but if you're a true fan of Steampunk, you probably like being a little technical!), and consider how to achieve great power the simple way: aether.

If your Storyteller allows aether in the game, it will certainly be a game-changer, as it will border on the magical. Because aether is a great unknown, we suggest that it be used as a means to an end result, and not in and of itself *the* end result.

So, if you have an aether-powered pistol, the aether itself does not shoot out of the gun and disintegrate your target. Instead, it might allow a sonic pulse or a laser blast to travel out of the gun (you see, something we can measure in game terms).

Legacy Tech Retrofitting

Before we run out of space, we want to say something also about retrofitting. Somewhere in your Story world, there might be old vehicles with their computer chips fried, or intact gasoline systems (but you just don't have any refined gasoline anymore). If only you had some way to attach another source of power to them...they would run!

Well, you do (and can)! You can attach gasifier systems to them or retrofit them to be powered with steam (bypassing their current engine).

This will take some time and ingenuity, to be sure, as well as resources (steel, welding perhaps, screws, coils and gears), but it will definitely be worth it.

We just want to mention that Reliability and Instability (and Power) rules will apply here, too. But those specifics, we'll leave to your intellect and the Storyteller's intuition (for s/he must keep balance in the game to give you a good experience). Just remember that if you can think of it, so can the wicked Personalities in the game who might try to one-up you after they see what you've done! And that's how it works. That's why technology is always improving, getting better, getting faster, getting smaller. And in Steampunk, you'll be right on the cutting edge!

Welcome to the Rat Race!

TRANSPORTATION

Stop! If you're not a Storyteller, you should not be in this part of the book (from this page forward). Be forewarned! You'll only ruin your own fun if you know the secrets in this section's pages and you're not the Storyteller.

At some point in the rebuilding of society, Inventors will have achieved connecting the towns again with steam-powered transportation, not altogether ignorant of past designs, and not without great expense.

The Steampunk era will itself evolve as time goes on and in its midst will have hybrid concoctions for every type of machine that makes people get to one place or another as quickly as possible. Not all of these contraptions will be safe or efficient, but they might actually work, if one can look past the spectacle of it in favor of the utility.

Not everything would have been completely destroyed of the Old World, and so it would be common in some places for townsfolk to enjoy Old World vehicles and airplanes, ships and trains, which have been retrofitted with steam technology that has enough power to turn their heavy parts.

But there will be some who avoid the old designs completely (especially if there is any question of radio-active contamination), preferring instead to design their own transportation machines.

We'll cover both methods in this short chapter.

Automobiles

Of course, at the beginning of Steampunk Era, people will revert to horse-drawn carts and carriages (provided, of course, that they can find any horses — or oxen, or camels, for that matter).

But after they recover their wits about them, they'll start to realize that all was not lost, and begin to retrofit what they can with what fuel they can (necessity if the mother of invention, as the saying goes).

Wood- or coal-powered vehicles using gasifiers (like from World War II) can be great additions to your Story. These are

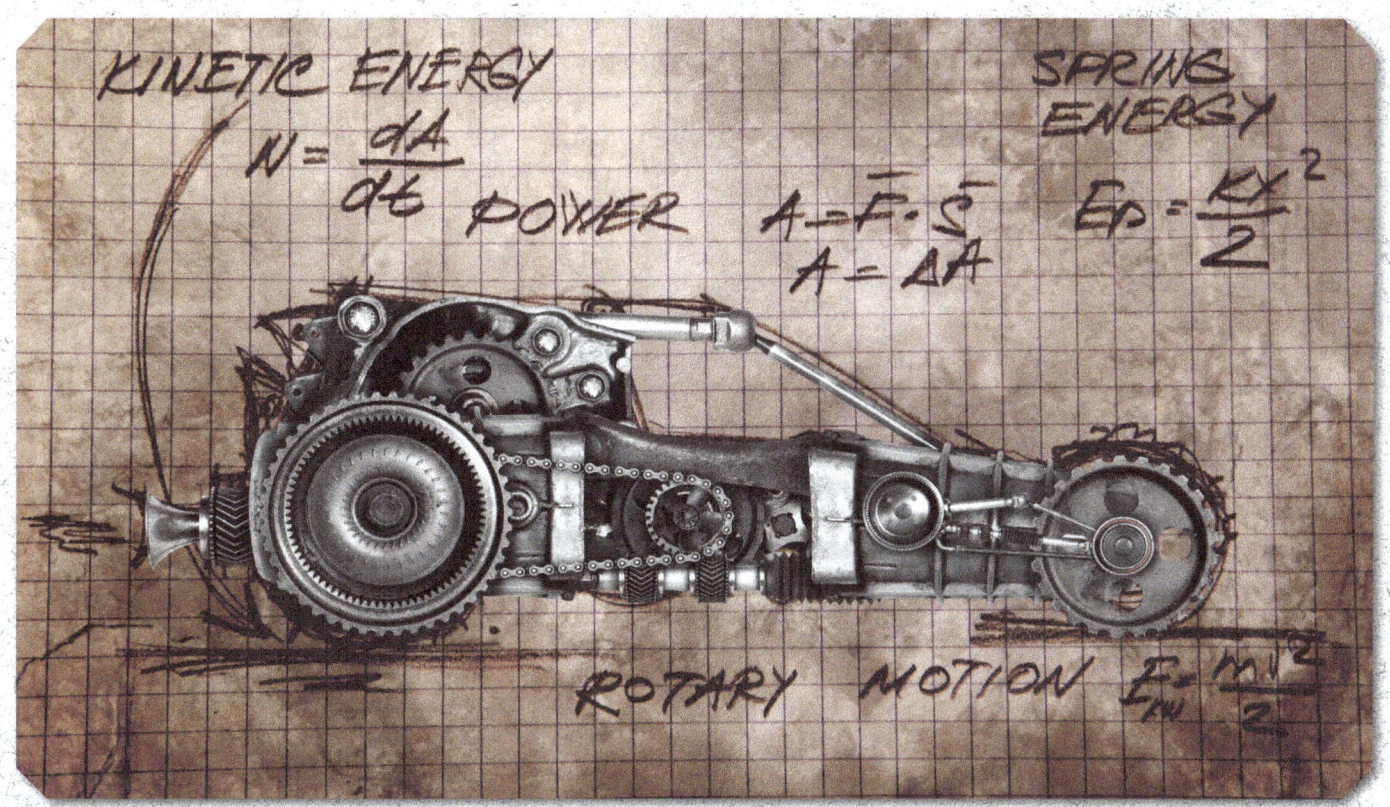

something any Inventor worth the title would be able to build, and then retrofit/attach Old World gas-powered engines. Here's a great video on it: https://youtu.be/3apnzNVHtLg (let us know if it doesn't work and we'll try to find a replacement video). It may also be worth noting that a gasifier can use just about anything that will burn as fuel (not just wood or coal).

A note of caution about the gasifiers. Remember the forests that might have gone up in flames because of the nukes? Well, there might be environmentalists who might vehemently object to your willy nilly throwing anything (and every type of endangered tree species into the oven). In fact, these radicals might even be a sure sign there are still nature-loving Arkadians ready to shapeshift and pounce on you before you can uproot the next sapling. Beware. "Treehugger" would be an understatement.

Of course, since it's Steampunk, water can be heated to make steam for retrofittings and new vehicle designs. For the truly adventurous Storyteller, retrofitting tanks and APCs is also possible.

Don't forget that many underdeveloped countries had to build bunkers deep underground for their very survival against those nuclear-capable nations. Therefore, they might be goldmines having fully functional cars, trucks, buses, tanks, fuel, oil, and maybe even some Meals Ready to Excrete.

Some real world examples of this include: North Korea's Pyongyang Metro (360 feet below ground) as well as the labyrinth of secret tunnels by the People's Army (these tunnels are large enough to drive tanks through them). Of course, if your Story had these areas specifically targeted during the EMP/Nuke war, then all bets are off.

Also, since there are broken cars everywhere in the big cities, it shouldn't be that hard to cannibalize for parts. Tires, though, might be a different story. Even if the rubber survived, good luck in finding a tire that isn't flat or ripped to threads, or rubber-rot-ridden.

Trains

Similarly, there are no steam engines left, except for the collectibles and some working models in countries that were never really able to enter into the advanced age the developed countries were able to enter. So, even spare parts will be extremely rare (and found in remote areas of the world).

For those wanting to make their own engines, either they will have to reinvent the wheel, have a book showing how, or

have the iron/steel available to retrofit existing (diesel-powered) wrecks. You can imagine, then, how valuable engineering books would become...

Of course, if you're really desperate, and don't care about the environment, you can always burn tires in your large-bellied steam/gasifier locomotives.

Now, even if you find a locomotives, you're going to have to drive it on something, and good luck finding a railway that doesn't have all of its bridges destroyed. Sleepers (railroad ties), rails, and spikes will probably all be scattered and reusable (well, not all the sleepers, anyway), if you are able to haul these heavy things around. If you only had a train to do it...

Under cities (yes the cities are probably contaminated with radiation, still) there may still exist some subway trains were built far enough underground so that they might be in functional order. It's just that they have no electricity to power them. Thus Explorers might have a quick way to get around 11-mile diameter cities if they can find a way to power them.

Oh, and let's not forget the subtropolis havens out there (do an Internet search for that word, we dare you) which might have working vehicles, train engines, semi-trucks, and diesel fuel to power your modern devices, at least for a while (all at your Storyteller Whim).

There would be long lines of railroad track that would still be intact, but there might be abandoned train cars sitting on them, serving to obstruct the path. Perhaps they are rusted apart. But a group of smart players needing to transport something heavy might try to look for something like this and then build their own worker car they can "pump" to make it go down the tracks.

Bottom line is that old steam locomotives and old boxcar trains can certainly lend a nice "setting" and nostalgia to your story.

Waterships and Submersibles

No Steampunk-o-phile would be able to forget the great story about Prince Dakkar (who? oh, Captain Nemo, thank you Jules Verne!) and his ship, the Nautilus. But that's a huge submarine full of mysterious advanced technology, which might fit your Story if Nemo is indeed an Ancient Atlantean Immortal masquerading as a Navigator.

Much more common would be the smaller pressurized tubular submersible that can fit only one, maybe two, people, and Explorers use these to see what they can discover and scavenge

from the deep hidden floors of lakes and oceans. These small devices might not even need any power source to propel them, being operated only by gears the passenger turns himself (if it has something like bicycle pedal-gear system). Quality manufacturing would be an absolute must, lest there be leaks resulting in death. Perhaps it would be wise to assign a Workmanship rating to these, just so you know when something might be leaking without being accused of unfairness...

As for above water ships, there might be some that are "dead in the water" — they survived the Nukes, but their innards are completely fried. These can be retrofitted, too, but their massive size would require a feat of engineering and money, not to mention other resources (steel, welding, etc.) that not many would have. Much more practical would be just to add a whole separate propulsion system so you wouldn't have to retrofit anything. Think tug-boat powered...

It would be kind of cool to have a "Steamtown" on a dead cruise ship, though...out in the middle of nowhere, hundreds of miles from any land, just drifting to wherever the currents take it. It is an idea more commonly used than one might think.

It is a fact that the British have long used decommissioned vessels (hulks) in order to house prisoners or soldiers. Imagine your Storyline if the players ran across one of these vessels containing one hundred murderers and thieves in them, who were just about to start feeding on each other to survive! What an amazing story hook that might be!

Airships

Or, if you like a more sophisticated word, Dirigibles. If you are in need of examples, we can go back to the massive Zeppelins of German fame. We can safely assume that most people do not realize how heavily these airships were used in the 1930s, and that would translate into heavy use in the Steampunk era, too.

For instance, the Editors of the Encyclopaedia Britannica report that "The Hindenburg, 804 feet long, was powered

by four 1100-horspower diesel engines, giving it a maximum speed of 84 miles per hour." The other zeppelin, only slightly more modest in fame, was the Graf Zeppelin, which, according to the same source, "had made 590 flights, including 144 ocean crossings, and had flown more than 1 million miles" prior to its "decommissioning in 1937."

It stands to reason, then, that dirigibles in our game setting would eventually be seen in greater and greater numbers, plied with Steam technology (or other type of gasifier) to avoid the flammable hydrogen that brought the Hindenburg down from its lofty perch. Whatever Steampunk town has command of dirigibles will have a huge leg-up over the rest, affording them significant military, trade, topographical, and communication advantages.

Aside from these types of dirigibles, we'll also see nice balloons aviators might enjoy using (see the great illustration at the end of the Magic & Aether section). It is likely the balloons

would actually be the first "re-invented" airships of the Steampunk era, and then gradually become more and more advanced so as to prove useful modes of transportation and sight-seeing.

Eventually, airplanes would be invented, but exactly when is completely up to you. If you want your Steampunk story to have flying aces battling each other, then go right ahead, just be conscious of fuel, oil, grease, and other things that might need to be readily available for such a story element.

We would suggest that as soon as your Story is getting ready to fit airplanes with jet engines, that you're at the end of the Steampunk era, so carefully ascertain exactly how much technology you're going to allow into your Steampunk game, as too much could ruin the feel pretty quickly.

In any case, leave some room for your Players to "invent" things. Perhaps they'll surprise you and start trying to find subtropolises without your slightest suggestion!

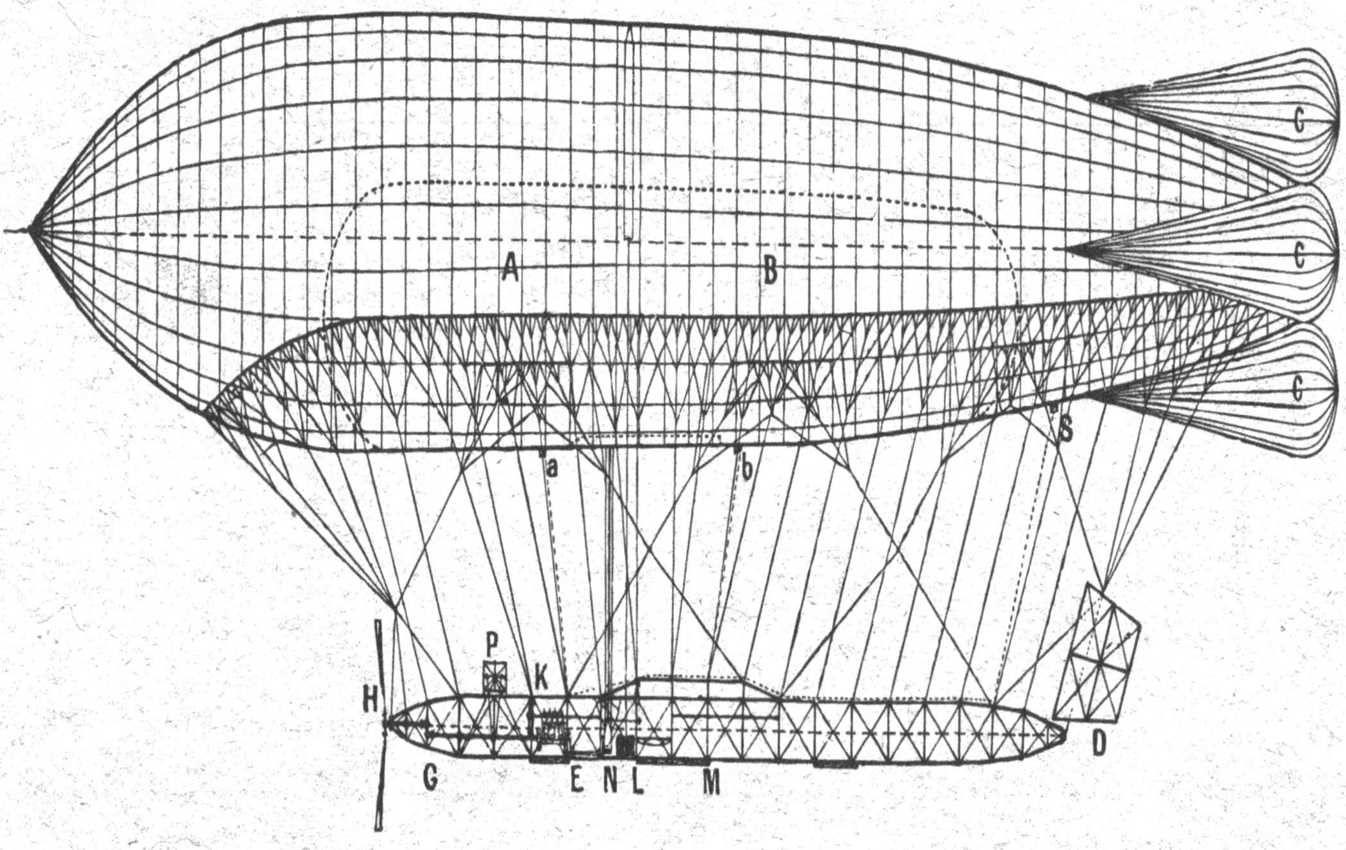

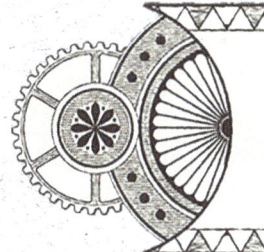

New Artifacts

Stop again! If you're not a Storyteller, you should not be in this part of the book (from this page forward). Be forewarned! You'll only ruin your own fun if you know the secrets in this section's pages and you're not the Storyteller.

Assuming you *are* the Storyteller, and not one of the Players, we'll be revealing some Steampunk secrets in Parts 7-9 of this booklet, specifically New Artifacts, a Bestiarium, and some pointers on how to make sure Immortal Empires' Steampunk stories remain different (superior?) to other steampunk RPGs, with your help!

The items that follow are by no means a complete list, but you should follow their example when populating your world with your own inventions.

Now that we are in the Steampunk era, having passed through the Dead Age and (now destroyed) first industrial revolution, not all artifacts are magical. Some will just have very useful, or unique, functions, and therefore may be highly sought after.

New Artifacts in Steampunk

In our Official Story, the Dead Age lasts for about seven hundred years (from 1360 to 2020 C.E.). That gives us enough time to reach the first Computer Age before the World War III EMP/Nuke war destroys most technological progress.

It also gives you some interesting centuries for you to run Adventures in some of your favorite historical settings, without magic if you desire.

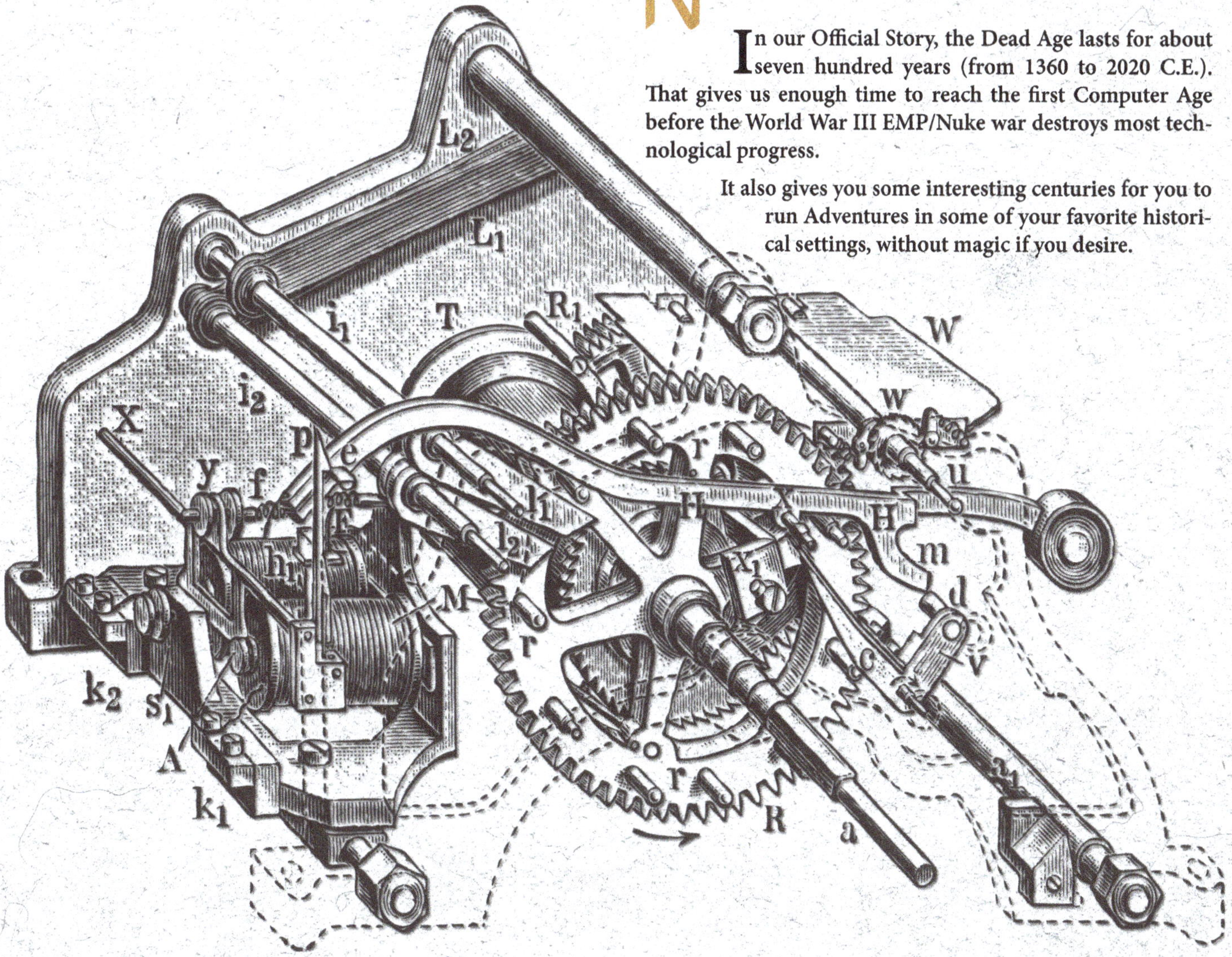

Odds are that some MenH items of the Seventh Age were simply lost or discarded by those who could no longer power them because of the belief that magic existed no more in the world. For example, a bale dagger without its magical healing property would be just about as good as any other knife, and perhaps not even as terror-inspiring as, say, a huge, curved hunting blade.

But there's the rub. Magic didn't die out, it died down. And the ever so small trickle of magic into the world would make MenH items precious still in the eyes of those who knew the truth.

Thus, over about 700 years, discarded MenH items would be buried in ancient cities, or by centuries of sand, or deep in the catacombs of modern cities built on top of older civilizations. And those cities would have been destroyed in the EMP war, or otherwise filled with radiation and beasts and the Overmind Cabal searching for those items.

The point is, there's justification for your players to find an artifact just about anywhere. Now whether there's any MTAP or MenH Binding still left on the item is all up to you.

Artifacts of the Seventh Age

SPHERETOWER FRAGMENT

Binding = None

Side Effect: Exposure Kills over Time

Aunt Julia's Circle of One Hundred Immortals was able to stop He Who Stands Alone and destroy that evil dracolich Sydyll by sending a couple of the Marune's Spheretowers to other Dimensions and by slicing through the two remaining ones with Original Magic.

Though no longer holding any magical binding, these fragments are still highly radio active and still made from Skydrop Metal. Since they a lot smaller than the entire Spheretower and Spheretower bowel, their radioactivity probably won't cause a desert...but they may kill everything within a garden-sized area, including, if left unshielded, a human exposed to it. The sickness will last several weeks (if the fragment is small (up to 8 Gy) with no cure short of using actual magic. Symptoms, including acute radiodermatitis will show up within 24 hours.

Vomiting, diarrhea, dizziness, and fever accompany radiation sickness, and for larger fragments, where exposure is 8 to 30 Gy, symptoms (including severe diarrhea) show up within an hour, and death in 2 to 14 days.

Even so, very small fragments might seem harmless, and allow a human carrier to avoid all symptoms of radiation sickness only to have them die from cancer after years of exposure.

Bottom line is that Spheretower fragments are dangerous artifacts that can only be used for ill in the Steampunk era, where in the Galactic Age, they might be able to serve as fuel boosters to Starships.

EYE OF SYDYLL

Binding = 340g   Activate: 2d10 MTAP for 20 minutes of use

Side Effect: Corrupts Wielder over Time

These things just refuse to be destroyed! Though Sydyll exploded because she got overrun by a Spheretower back in the Spheretower Cataclysm, her eyes survived, propelled by the explosion far away from the battlefield.

However, the explosion did change the Eyes magically as follows:

The Dyd Eye: no longer traps souls but can shrink from 5 inches down to the size of a human eye and can "replace" a normal eye (but if ever taken out, the natural eye must be grown back with MenH-g or BenH-n/p (BioTech -nano/-pico). If merely held, the Dyd Eye can be used as a source for Pure Negative Energy. If it is inserted into an eye socket, the person will be able to see all MenH items since they will "glow" to his Dyd Eyesight.

The Shattered Eye: No longer does this eye reveal all the disguises someone looked at has worn, but it does reveal whether someone is failing to tell the truth as they speak.

Each eye has a corrupting influence but can only corrupt up to 20% of a person's life force (MTAP) for purposes of corruption rolls (where the person loses his/her inhibitions and does something socially unacceptable or violent). If both eyes are held or installed in one person's eye sockets, then the total corruption is 40%.

If both eyes are installed in one person (or golem), the person has a 10% chance per day (non-cumulative) of "becoming" Sydyll the Dracolich in mind only (without the ability to actually be a Dracolich), and will probably be seen as having gone "mad." However, the person using both Eyes in his own eye sockets at the same time, gains these abilities: [1] he can force someone he stares at to lie (speak untruth) in the manner he

desires MAF OPPROLL; [2] he is able to see magic as per Third Eye +5 (schools, inverted magic, etc.).

FRAGMENT OF THE GREAT PLINTH

Binding = 1g   Activate: 1d10 MTAP to use 1 time

Side Effect: Effect might backfire on user

When the Newborn Races were finally able to overrun the Astorian Empires in the Dead Age (and the Astorians went into hiding with the rest of the Ancient Races), Rhodes was not spared. The Great Plinth that had for so long given Master Scholars their highly magical rings had died with Aunt Julia way back at the end of the Seventh Age, becoming, for all practical purposes just a big rock. The Newborn hordes chiseled and hammered it apart in their zealous vengeance into hundreds of jagged, shard-like fragments, some the size of a short sword, some as small as a fist.

However, after several centuries, these fragments somehow regained a very small magical property, having for so long been a direct gateway (when it was the Great Plinth) to the Brilliance Dimension. As such, they now are able to serve as a conduit to that Dimension, but which way the magic will flow is anyone's guess.

Each fragment, at each use, has a 60% chance to drain any user's MTAP (down to zero) completely into itself all the way to the Brilliance Dimension, that MTAP forever lost. But there is also a 39% chance (61 to 99) that the conduit goes the other way, filling the user with exactly as much MTAP as the percentage they rolled (if 61 to 99). If the user rolls a percentile CRIT (100), they get to roll a CRIT Multiplier (d5) and thus can receive up to 5x100 (500) MTAP, depending upon the d5 roll.

In each and every case, the fragment is destroyed.

VESTAL VIRGIN DRESS

Binding = 5g   Activate: 1d10 MTAP for 24 hour use

Side Effect: Restores Virginity (Physically)

Even clean, these dresses are no longer in style, and any High Society madam attempting to wear one would be soundly ridiculed by the other Ladies, but a servant or commoner might be able to get away with it. Nobility is not always easily seen and it is so with these dresses (of which there are no more than 12 in existence).

Once donned and activated, the dress immediately heals any virginal damage (for a woman; upon a man this side effect does

nothing), with a permanent healing (until it is broken again). Also, the wearer is able to hear the surface thoughts of anyone within her MAF x Hexes, so long as they are not trying to hide them from her (i.e., by using some type of synergistic, magical or BioTech-enhanced mind shielding to avoid mind-reading powers).

If they do have a defense against mind-reading, then the dress affords an automatic OPPROLL (whether or not the wearer wants to hear their thoughts). The strength of the mind-reading ability is MAF x d10, and the OPPROLL goes directly against their shielding strength, bypassing any and all bodily MResist.

ARVAL RING

Binding = 1g   Activate: 1d10 MTAP for 1 hour use

Side Effect: None

When activated, these rings (which can be of any metal, as there were several secret societies within the Arval Brotherhood (Flamines, etc.) change from a ring into some type of medieval sword commonly used by the Arvals: gladius, spatha, legionnaire's axe, and in rare cases, even an 8-foot long Astorian Great Sword (two-handed). It can be willed back into a ring at any time, or will naturally change itself back into a ring once its duration has run.

While some of these rings have probably been lost throughout the 8th Age, and therefore able to be found, it is doubtful that the Arval Master Ring has been lost, and is most likely proudly worn by the current Astorian Emperor/Empress (even though they remain in hiding far from the suspicious eyes of the Newborn races).

Artifacts of the Eighth Age

ANCIENT OSHEKOGAN SECRET

Binding = None

Side Effect: Impotence

Explosive black powder, made with saltpeter, sulfur, and charcoal is the ancient Oshekogan secret, but we're talking more about a couple of the old applications of that powder that might have survived (and may still be useful in the Steampunk era). While handling black powder may not cause impotence, consuming it, or more accurately, consuming the saltpeter, will over time.

Gunpowder bombs: old handheld grenade or larger ball-like containers shot by catapults, with burning fuses the cut to the length of time the bomb needs to reach its target. These can also contain shrapnel which yield +2/die damage. Generally, each inch of diameter yields 1d10 damage in that many Hexes (so a 5-inch diameter bomb would yield 5d10 damage to a radius of 5 Hexes (yards)).

Fire cannon: a flaming missile fired from a bamboo or metal tube. Causes the same damage, but has a further range than hand thrown. For weak tubes, like bamboo, the range is 50 yards. For metal tubes the range could be as far as 250 yards.

Fireworks: colorful explosives meant for entertainment, these come in all manner of sizes, and usually have a wick and propulsion component to get them up into the sky, where they can explode into many different colors and designs as the fiery explosions burn different elements/chemicals to create colors and effects. These are usually very expensive items, and the Chemists that make them are usually very wealthy, so long as they do not have to pay their Explorers too much money for finding the base cursors they need.

Finally, it would be extremely rare that these artifacts have survived not getting wet (and thereby dissolving the water-soluble saltpeter), so if you stumble across some that have survived, make sure you don't ruin them yourself by trying to use them in the rain.

SPINNING JENNY

Binding = None

Side Effect: None

A small to mid-sized machine, the Spinning Jenny will no doubt make a come back during the Steampunk era, and it is likely to be fitted with ornate steam engine power, eventually. The Spinning Jenny facilitates weaving threads into fabric.

DYNAMITE

Binding = None

Side Effect: Premature explosions/failure to explode

While there may certainly be some Chemists out there that will still make nitroglycerin, they'll charge a premium for the more stable dynamite. Each stick of dynamite, when it works (W70), has a blast radius of 10 Hexes and does 15T15 damage.

THE FLINT LOCK

Binding = None

Side Effect: Missfire and Explosion

While nobody would use a flintlock handgun or rifle while better weapons are available. But early in the Steampunk era, they might be the only weapons around (especially if they are actually Pre-war advanced weapons that were retrofitted out of necessity).

Of serious concern when using an older (or jury-rigged) weapon, is the Workmanship rating, and that depends on your Storyteller. If you roll above that rating, the weapons will missfire and either just go "Click" or explode, maiming your hand (and if you were aiming closely, your eyes, too).

Artifacts that Survived the Nukes

These items will be extremely hard to find and probably only available OFF GRID. Some of them might even still have radioactivity from nuke fallout, so beware, as the places most likely to have these kinds of things were probably targeted by bona fide hydrogen nukes and not mere EMPs.

We give a few here to set the stage, but your Storyteller will have more (or less), depending on how s/he is telling your story.

But we also want to emphasize that in our Official Storyline, most of the earth, for several years after the Nuke War, suffers from Nuclear Winter, meaning no crops and mostly frozen and contaminated water sources. The UV radiation that penetrates the 150 million tons of smoke that envelopes the earth would further kill crops.

But 5-10 years after the cataclysm, temperatures would begin to approach normal again, things would attempt to grow green, and the smoke will have settled. Droughts would finally end as rain (other than acid rain) would again fall on the earth.

Perhaps some natural features (wind patterns, mountains, proximity to oceans) might lengthen drought or nuke winter in

some areas well into 20+ years past the Nuke War. But all that is up to your Storyteller to tell you.

We just don't want you to get the idea that everything is happy go lucky in Steampunk. Quite to the contrary, it is dangerous, and the mindset of the survivors (especially First Generation survivors though it wanes as time marches on) is wholly about surviving at all costs...even if you're the one they must sacrifice!

PLASTIC EXPLOSIVES (C-4, H-6)

Binding = None

Side Effect: Radiation Sickness if exposed

Extremely rare and found only in radiation-contaminated zones, plastic explosives do not ignite by mere contact with fire but must have a spark. Thus, only the most well-informed Explorer or Chemist will even know what the soft substance is.

Each pound of this "heavy" plastic has an explosive radius of 4 Hexes, but does a whopping 25T25 damage to everything within that radius, meaning most Newborn and Starborn would die instantly from the blast. Momentum (carried by the shock wave) is 10 x Damage rolled. So, if you wish to figure out how fast things fly out from the explosion based on their mass (Momentum = Mass x Velocity), you can and from there you can figure out how far they would have traveled.

For example if the rolled damage was 60, the Momentum would equal 600. Therefore, a 200 pound person would take 60 damage to each body part and be knocked back 3 Hexes (more, if some of that damage was resisted by armor). On a typical being, this example would leave that person with no arms and no legs (they will have been blown the fuck off), and no head, unless s/he were an Ancient Race with the Vitals protection (head & torso are one).

Since H-6 was an explosive composition used mainly for underwater explosions (although it was used for the Mother of All Bombs (MOAB) as well), we deem it to have probably survived the war in some remote or desolate places.

HAND GRENADE

Binding = None

Side Effect: Unstable Fuse when pulled: W85

Here, we're talking about a normal frag grenade having a kill radius of 5 Hexes and a shrapnel radius of about 15 Hexes. Damage is 15T15 in the kill radius and 15T15-1/Hex outside the kill radius (so if a person was 8 Hexes away from the exploding Hex, that would be 3 (8-5=3), which would translate into 15T12 (15-3=12) damage. Thus, at 15 Hexes away from the epicenter, the damage would be 15T0 (no damage). Other types of grenades will have survived, too: smoke, white phosphorous, concussion, incendiary, colored smoke, riot control (CS gas, tear gas), stun, and of course practice grenades (which still might work as black powder grenades if rigged).

ARMORED VESTS

Binding = None

Side Effect: A vest could be faulty and only have W60

Happy the Explorer who finds an armored vest intact and undamaged. While the exact terminology of the ballistic materials used for it might be lost to all but the most learned of sages, it is still evident that these vests can stop all manner of projectiles and in some cases knife attacks.

Of course, it would be a serious offense for anyone to display laughable paranoia by wearing such a thing to a High Society dinner party, and any Constable would surely envy a commoner found to have an armored vest (and perhaps arrange for that commoner to be arrested so that he could "confiscate" the commoner's belongings).

ADVANCED SMALL ARMS AND MUNITIONS

Binding = None

Side Effect: Some munitions might missfire W70

While there certainly may be some that survived, they would be in ultra-high demand, since most of them (and the ammunition as well) would have been used and destroyed during the World War, as nukes targeted armies and fleets.

SCUD-B MISSILE

Binding = None

Side Effect: Might missfire if still working W65

Depending on the one you were lucky enough to find, a SCUD-B is about 37 feet long and almost 3 feet in diameter and has a blast radius of 160 to 250 Hexes, has a range of 300000 Hexes. With fuel and warhead (that weighs about 2000 lbs), the SCUD will weigh about 7000 lbs. Of course, nuclear warheads will increase the blast radius significantly. Damage is, at a minimum, 100T100 x 5 to everything within the blast radius.

Nuclear warheads would multiply this blast radius and damage (100T100 x 5) by a factor of 10 to 100, depending on the type of nuke (ensuring the death of even lower level Immortals,

as all of their Immortal ranks would have been destroyed, too).

Of course, it's not much use if it doesn't have a launcher and an intact targeting system, and if it hasn't exploded by now, it's probably a dud anyway, unless it's rigged to discourage off greedy Scavengers exploring places they shouldn't be snooping around in...

New Artifacts of Steampunk Fame

You'll be able to come up with much better artifacts of your own, we're sure, but just to get you started, we've dropped a couple here from our Official Storyline.

Often, Steampunk artifacts will have all sorts of replicas and "fakes" floating around, and there's usually only one "real" item, and if there are more, it's probably still owing to only one truly gifted Inventor (or one who has stumbled across a MenH item he was able to fuse into his machine).

This is why we've named a few of these, to make them truly unique. There might be other steam powered typewriters out there, but does the carriage all fly off the track at 30 mph? Nope, only Johnson's typewriters can do that...

Also, some strange typewriter machines might not be typewriters at all, but encoders, like the Enigma Machine, which allowed people to communicate secretly so long as their cipher was known only to them. Having such a machine would be a huge advantage for any OFF GRID criminal organization plotting against another; even if couriers were captured, confiscated plans would not be compromised.

As seen in the illustration above, the fancier typewriters are connected via hose to a steam compressor which allows for an effortless carriage return and effortless typing. A pressure gauge helps the user make sure that [1] enough pressure is present for an automatic return, and [2] not too much pressure is present (upon which time a valve should be operated in order to reduce the pressure...Or Not. Perhaps the typewriter is also a weapon where the carriage can fly off its track upon an over-pressured carriage return, hit the target in the head, and the whole event can be chalked up to a grave accident....Of course, it could also be used to knock loose a bad tooth, perhaps?

Johnson's Personal Typewriter Machine

Binding = None

Side Effect: None, or Maybe just what the doc ordered...

The electric typewriters would have been destroyed. But, there still may be some older typewriters out there that were in museums or the like, and in various languages. It wouldn't be too difficult to make your own spooling ribbons that contain ink.

Dr. Huckleberry's Golden Gun MK III

Binding = None

Side Effect: 50% Steam release

This beauty has several useful functions, both when plugged into a steam source and when not, provided that there is still pressurized air inside (hasn't been used yet). It uses non-black powder bullets only (being only steam-propelled).

Steam Source Active. While plugged into a steam source, Huckleberry's Golden Gun is able to shoot seriously burning

steam streams up to 15 feet away, causing 3T2 damage from steamy burns (this stream would come out of the lower barrel. If the victim is within 3 feet (adjacent Hex), then the steam causes 3T3 damage.

Second, the gun is able to fire the round it has in the chamber (High Velocity impact) for 4T4-50 Hex. Rounds must be loaded from the right side one at a time. Bullets or balls can be used, so long as their size matches snugly the .44 caliber this chamber requires.

Third, the gun can be fired backwards by using the bullet attached at the top, but this bullet only has an effective range of 5 Hexes for 3T3 damage. (Hence the user can appear to be turning the gun on himself and still kill his enemy, so long as he pushes the correct button and does not pull the trigger and by accident kill himself!).

Steam Source Not Attached. So long as the gun previously had a steam source attached (within 12 hours), there will be enough pressure held in the gun for exactly one shot, either with the .44 round chamber, or with the reverse bullet. Of course, there will be no steam attack stream, either.

The side effect might happen only when loading the weapon if there is a steam source attached (and active). There's a 50% chance that the chamber won't open exactly right (or quick enough) allowing a small bit of steam to escape while loading. This amount of steam is sufficient to burn the skin and force the loader to drop the round he was loading. Wearing gloves isn't really a solution, because the gloves would not allow the manipulation required to get the round into the chamber and then press the chamber release to lock it in. But, there might be other ways to avoid this side effect.

Margo's Magic Goggles

Binding = None

Side Effect: Temporary Blindness if used wrongly

The name implies that there is some magic to these goggles, and one might be persuaded that magic truly does exist when they put them on, but really, they're just a really nice invention.

The goggles can be charged with a bit of steam to pressurize both of the chambers which propel the gears that rotate the lenses within the goggles. That's all the steam does. If there is no steam, the lenses can still be rotated, but not in a simple click, and will take much longer.

At the top of each goggle, there is a button one can push

to rotate that side's lens. If the middle button is pressed at the same time, one of the side buttons will rotate both eyes' lenses at once, keeping them synced. If not, then each goggle will rotate its lens only when that side's top button is pushed.

The 50mm (aperture) goggles have three functions: telescopic sight (4x, 8x, 10x, and 20x, so four lenses stacking); microscopic sight (4x, 10x, 20x), and shading (3 settings: clear, sunscreen (like sunglasses — not meant to look directly into the sun), and welding screen).

Temporary blindness can occur in two ways with these goggles: [1] looking directly into the sun, even when using the welding screen; [2] mis-matching telescopic lenses in one eye with microscopic lenses in the other eye. While this might be acceptable on the small scale (the goggles have 10 lenses in each side) to correct nearsighted/farsighted mismatched eyes, extreme lenses should be avoided.

It takes a Free PhAct to press the lens button up to two times (so long as there is enough pressure to turn the lens); otherwise, manual turning of the lens takes a 1/2-PhAct. If primed, the goggles can rotate lenses with the buttons 20 times before the pressure runs out.

Finally, Margo's Magic Goggles come with a spring-loaded clip on each side so that the goggles can be attached to helmets, masks, or lab stands.

Their worth is nearly priceless to the serious Inventor, Chemist, or even Explorer/Scavenger who needs to see far away places for safe travels.

SAGATH'S STEAM POWERED ELECTRIC MIND

Binding = None

Side Effect: Unknown

Probably near the end of the Steampunk era, an Inventor will invent this bit of awesome technology, with wires running from it to all over the place, with photo-tubes transferring their signals to the machine. Perhaps it is only something that allows a person to type their own telegram. Perhaps, this machine is much, much, more. Only you, Storyteller, can decide that!

A FEW THINGS TO CONSIDER

As you start making your own artifacts, remember that even a household item can be an artifact in the Steampunk era. Either the item is a barely functioning treasure from the Old World (that is, the industrially advanced civilization that existed before the EMP/Nuke blasts), or the item is "retro-fitted" in such a way as to have a hidden function that it's not really supposed to have. The more inventive you can get with this, the more your players will be impressed.

Also, try to limit the availability of artifacts; they shouldn't be so common as to be not valued highly by the players. In the Steampunk era, any machine that affords even the slightest advantage or bit of one-uppedness can be highly sought after by all manner of Personalities.

Finally, be meticulous on what you're presenting (perhaps do some research) as your world's story. In the above picture, would they really have nice white paper yet? Or would vellum, or parchment, be a better choice? It depends on your Story.

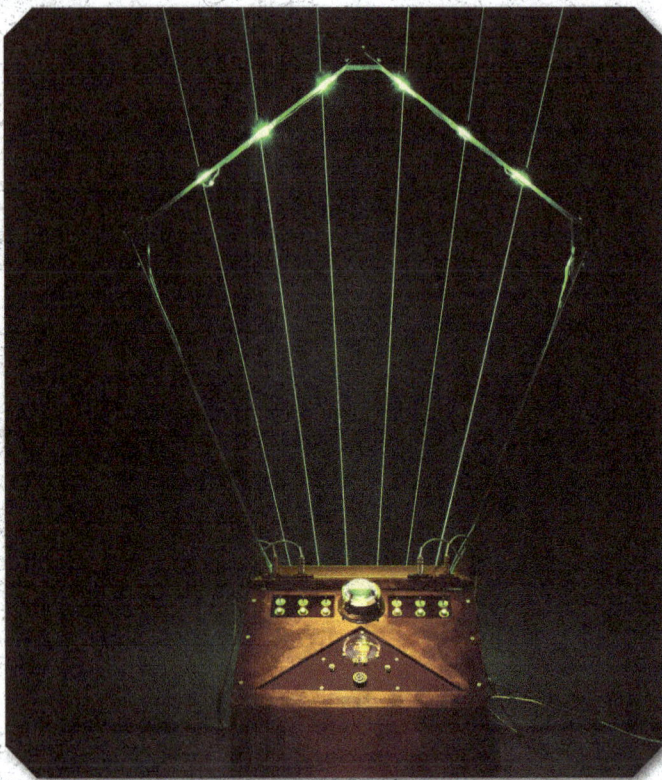

SAGATH'S ELYSIUM HARP

Binding = None

Side Effect: Unknown

This harp is the envy of every Mayor that knows about it. Run entirely by steam, which turns a small turbine for electricity, the harp has powerful lenses concentrating the light into lasers which pass a reflective arch above. When the beams are disrupted (and thus do not reflect), the machine plays a pleasant organ-like sound through pipes within the box (also powered by steam).

While there might be other Laser Harps by other inventors, only Sagath's harps have the ability to "play" a hard-coded wheel which has holes and multicolored lenses that effectively block and/or recolorize the lasers so that a song is automatically played along with a brilliant colorful light show.

Often used as a prize among Mayors during a friendly Olympics-style series of tournaments, the machine has also caused fatal jealousy to break out among them. It could be said that the Harp is enchanting, soothing, while it plays, and the loss of it creates a murderous desire to recover it. Owners have been known to have their favorite Song Wheel, as well.

BESTIARIUM

PART EIGHT

What would an Immortal Empires rules expansion be without some additional bad guys and devious Personalities? After all, manipulative Personalities are our bread and butter for a great and exciting game, right? It is our humble opinion that the intrigue caused by intelligent Personalities who may or may not be working against your players' personal ambitions (whether purposely or by accident) is ever so much more fun than "kill the goblins with my spear and magic helmet" type of game.

If you're playing Immortal Empires, we know you agree!

So one thing up front about Steampunk personalities: they are archetypally small-minded, aspiring to no higher thought than perhaps being Mayor of the town someday, or king of the town's Off Grid underground. We will leave it to the players and perhaps some Major Personalities to consider the bigger picture (i.e., empire building).

Keeping that in mind, you'll easily see then, how the High Society Ladies of the town think no further than tomorrow's tea party and the gossip they'll spread during it.

Once the players discover this, they might think that the townsfolk will be easily manipulated to their own ends, and perhaps they will be, but if you're the great Storyteller we know you to be, you'll have your superior Personalities interpret the players' words/actions/manipulations in a way as to let that Personality help/hinder with their own manipulations on their smaller-minded ambitions.

Every once in a while, you'll be able to throw in that mastermind Personality who is also trying to become Emperor/Empress. If you do it right, the Players will never know which Personality is the Mastermind until it is too late, and they're already at a great disadvantage against which they'll have to work together to overcome.

We'll start with the Major Personalities first this time, and then go to the Monsters, and then finally to the minor personality chart that you can use to quickly populate your story on the fly for unexpected interactions during game play.

Finally, remember that you are the Storyteller. You can change these personalities any way you choose. Make them Immortal, make them Ancient Races, or even make them Overmind Cabal sleeper agents! Make them have secret lives, secret wives, off grid debts, et cetera et cetera! In short, make them

your own, and then tell us about them in our Immortal Empires forums!

We want to hear everything about your own Storytelling, and maybe even other Storytellers will be able to benefit from your wily inventiveness!

Why we don't include STATS

The new Major Personalities we describe in the following pages should be customizable for your Story. While it certainly stands to reason that Mayors should be somewhat powerful, that might not always be the case. It could be that your Mayor is only *perceived* to be powerful because she's a great philanthropist, but in all actuality, she's a wimp! Perhaps she doesn't even have her ORANK up to one yet, and all of her Main Attributes are still at ZERO! But she has several Traits that make her sound important (like the E.F. Hutton Syndrome trait), or beautiful, etc.

Yes, indeed! Perhaps she has hunks all around her who are the true power behind the throne, and they're all captivated by her in one way or another such that their allegiance to her is unwavering.

Better yet, perhaps the Mayor doesn't even know why people support him, but the High Society and Constables all do... Because, unbeknownst to him, they are all Overmind Cabal! They need him, and subtly direct him, to be the "legitimate storefront" for Overmind's reaching into that territory. Visitors to this town would probably sense that there was something strange going on, but wouldn't be able to put their finger on it.

Also, remember that you can have some of the Major Personalities from the Storyteller's Codex as having survived (being Immortals) the Dead Age, and perhaps they are Mayors or Chief Constables (so that they don't have to be the "face" of the town) who are content hiding their true identities and power until the Age evolves to where they can come out of hiding (the Cyber Age). Your Players should be very powerful if you're going to have them interact with Immortals; otherwise you might have to invent reasons why your Immortals won't just squish them, especially if they become suspicious and start blabbing that the Immortal isn't who s/he says s/he is...

Finally, remember that Marunes still roam about, seeking to guide mankind to destruction, and deprive the Presidium of their Star Legions. Of course, no one believes in them....

MAYOR GÜNTHER BLUMFELD

Günther Blumfeld is a rather manipulative and offensively funny Personality to introduce to your Players, and you should carefully consider whether doing so will offend them, as Günther is an in-your-face flaming eccentric.

Günther uses his vast experience and knowledge to create esoteric insults framed as hilarious "joking around." He has an extremely colorful repertoire full of jokes, insults, personal anecdotes and knows how to use them with blatant and unashamed innuendo.

"That's not what you said last night when you were moaning, 'GÜNTHER, GÜNTHER, deeper, please!" You'll regret becoming his target, even if he considers you a friend. And don't let him get drunk. All bets are off then, and no one is safe, High Society etiquette notwithstanding.

Really, though, Günther is very self-conscious and abuses his friends and enemies with witty, crude and not-so-friendly humor to mask his insecurities about his smaller stature, skin condition (eczema "I don't know what soap I'm using that does this! Charlatans!"), and homely mug...he loves his goggles!

His trade, besides sex and the manipulation that is involved at all stages with this — the Hunt, the Conquest, and the Morning After — is knowledge. He is king of one-night stands, but instead of being done with you the morning after, he uses intimate morsels about you to make you vulnerable to his control.

He never gets angry, except when his inner clique betrays him, either by gossiping about him behind his back, taking his gifts without returning friendship (he's more apt to make you the butt of all his jokes at the next High Society party). Otherwise, he just likes to get even by making you look like a fool in front of everyone. And then, when he's done chewing you to pieces he'll leave you broken for the rest of the wolves to devour.

Nobody understands how he's Mayor since he insults everyone all the time. Nobody knows how he maintains power or respect among his peers, but he's very comfortable being Mayor, very apt, and very protective of that title.

He owns a lot of old shit that reminds him of a life (or many) he ruminates absentmindedly and intermittently about it all. In other words, his house looks like a Victorian pawn shop: everything has dust on it but where did he and it all come from?

No one *ever* finds out exactly what Günther is hiding.

MADAM SYLVIA HURST

Personality Quick Look

Deportment

Braggadocious, self-important. She considers herself the most intelligent person in the room and loves to argue.

Temperament

Like a firecracker. Anything she perceives as lack of respect raises her ire immediately. She has wit and a sword for a tongue and will out-banter many.

Past Sins

Maintains that she is a virgin and will zealously guard her honor: 5 new husbands (now deceased) who thought they could bed her before she was ready.

Future Goals

To become Mayor of 3 or 10 towns, keep her "virginity" and rule forever.

The leader of the entire High Society clique in her town, Madam Sylvia Hurst is a five-time widow at only twenty-seven years old (but it would not be a good idea to remind her of either that or her age). While it seems that she appreciates men wooing her, as well as their polite admiration, she is loathe to give in to their lustful base desires, preferring instead to keep herself pure (and her heart ultimately unfettered).

Independence is the very reason all the rest of the Ladies look up to her (even while the common wives think she's an embarrassment to their town for the unladylike, manly role she takes on). Occasionally, she'll be caught walking in her private garden wearing her late husbands' heavy shirts. Some even spread the false rumors that these are the very shirts they died in. It goes without saying that she is very wealthy, having been the sole beneficiary of all her hubbies' grand possessions.

Sylvia knows how people ruthlessly gossip about her past and does just fine ignoring all those stares and whispers while she is conducting herself around town. But she will remember every single one of them...for later.

The drama she weaves in High Society circles gets so terrible that usually someone has to die before the injured party feels satisfied; Sylvia is very good at making people hate each other while she herself continues to be idolized by the High Society Ladies. Many loathe her, but they would never let it show.

Even when she is bedding their husbands, she's quick to point out that it must have been that wench Maudine since, "Oh, looky here, this is Maudine's hairpin! Pray tell, Lydia, what is it doing in your husband's coat jacket?"

So, you see, Sylvia learned all about supply and demand from her bevy of deceased husbands (more than one of whom were rumored to be Charlatans). If there is no demand, you need to create it! And demand for her is high off grid...

That's why she is so successful as The Clipper, an assassin of indeterminate sex that deals solely in word-of-mouth recommends. She stirs up townsfolk against each other by her High Society tea parties, dinners, and of course, little bits of gossip to the town merchants and barbers, all to create enough hatred among them so that someone will eventually put the correct type of ad in the town paper, and The Clipper can get paid.

Of course, the word-of-mouth recommends are easily suggested by her own mouth to the lady seeking to hire an assassin to take out her cheating husband and his lover.

LUTHER LOCKETT, II

Luther is quite content being the Chief Constable of the town, a town he would love to be called Luckettville some day. He's made no secret about this, but never makes any move openly or secretly to usurp power from his Mayor.

Notwithstanding his loyalty to the Head Man/Woman, his detractors (and there are many among the common and High Society gossips alike) call him "Bucketswill" behind his back. Thus far, he hasn't let on that he knows anything about that, and most people think that he would go ape-shit if he did, so they speak of him like that only in whispers.

As chief constable, he wears many hats: investigator, arresting officer, chief of security for the Mayor, lead surveillance officer, forensic specialist, chief of ceremonies, and, when the act is justified by the Town's law: executioner.

He doesn't have time for love, and besides, he's convinced that anyone who approaches him that way is doing so only to get him to turn a blind eye to violations of the law, and that he simply can not allow. He will not bend. He is unyielding. He is relentless. He would pursue the pettiest lawbreaker to the Dead Cities and hell itself if he could spare time away from his myriad municipal duties.

He is often, therefore, dismayed that his employees (the lesser constables) are always up to something behind his back. He will catch them one day, and if the Mayor doesn't have mercy on them, Luther the Executioner will be happy to wear that hat for a while.

It doesn't occur to Luther that his distrust and zeal has in reality depleted his ability, not enhanced it. It doesn't occur to him that he barely has enough time to shop for a second pair of boots, let alone catch every crime committed, because of all the hats he has to keep wearing at all different parts of the day. It doesn't occur to him that no one, except other OCD or overzealous weirdos really would work under him or carry out his orders to the letter. In short, Luther is his own worst enemy.

Of course, there probably are constables working under him who compromise themselves, especially when it comes to High Society crimes. These types readily accept Luther's abuse and jump to obey, so as to not come under suspicion.

Luther is quick to confront anyone (except the Mayor, who, of course, *is* the law) when he thinks a crime may have been committed, High Society rank notwithstanding. He'll soon find out the truth of every matter, especially for the Mayor's safety.

BARONESS SYNTHIA MOOREHEAD

Synthia Moorehead is on the run and if asked why, it's because her father wants her to live a boring life as a Baroness at his huge estate. He often sends his men looking for her to bring her back, she claims, so if you could just help her out a little, buy her miracle elixirs and little contraptions, she'll have enough dough to keep free of the tyrant! Oh, and by the way, if you could just risk your life and duel with that man over there... he's one of my father's henchman and he's been stalking me. I'll make it worth your while...as she smiles and rubs her bare leg.

Synthia — Syn for short — travels light, only one suitcase, perhaps an extra purse, and of course some nice surprises under her hat, just in case. She makes her living making your life happier, replacing your frown with a smile, giving you hope against all your ailments and pains. The very strong alcoholic "medicines" she sells will do nicely, while she steals what she can stuff into her paltry belongings in order to continue her adventure —

— or flight, actually. Syn has several (dozen?) men pursuing her, stalking her since she promised them marriage, and some of those men are already married! So, occasionally, you'll have a woman or two (wives of those men) stalking her to *take back* the jewelry or money she ran off with (and in some rare cases, to get more absinthe from her because they became addicted).

But of course, she doesn't know what they're talking about when it comes to their accusations (and besides, she sold all of her knick knacks just to get fare for the train and grub). You should feel sorry for her! If all the accusations were true, she'd be living in a mansion by now, wouldn't she?

But the simple fact is, Syn loves life, and spends anything she "earns" as quickly as she gets it on life's pleasures (for herself, of course, and temporary friends who remain strangers as she's up before dawn thumbing her way out of town).

She knows a lot of people, so if you ever do cross her, she can be a very bad enemy, or if you treat her right, she might know just the person you need to meet, the town you need to go to, and the right road to take to avoid the bandits and trolls that hide in every bush and under every bridge.

Even while she flees, she knows how to manipulate the fanatical men that stalk her, and maybe she will promise a smile or dainty morsel to them, so long as they do her bidding. So do not think you are safe by allying yourself with them against her.

BRAN HICKBURN, AVIATOR

Personality Quick Look

Deportment

Suave and loves to be the center of attention, acts braver than he really is. Keeps the conversation about what he knows: airships, aviation, and leather.

Temperament

Passive aggressive with anger, as he is more cowardly than brave. Runs away from a fight, especially from a jealous husband when sweet talking the wife.

Past Sins

For all the hype, is still probably a virgin and lacks confidence. Smuggler, murderer, scavenger.

Future Goals

Bigger and more luxurious airships, aether powered, and all the ale he can...

Bran blames his last name as the reason he's never gotten married; no woman wants to be called Mrs. Hickburn, and it's been his experience that women love his sky-high tales of grandeur and success until they learn what is last name is.

So, he' changed it countless times, and every time he's changed it, he's done something truly phenomenal, like crossing the Alps without crashing, or narrowly escaping crashing into the sea when one of his airship's steam pipes burst, to the amazement of all who were watching him fly off. And so, all of those Brans got the glory, and they got the fame. It is their name the bards sing. But Bran Hickburn? Who's he but a story teller of other people's adventures.

He'd like to someday be the one who's famous, but his aspirations require off grid work. In order to afford the most powerful and luxurious skyliner in the world — perhaps even invent aether power himself — he's going to need a lot, and he means a lot, of money.

So, of course, he's partner to smugglers off grid. He'll even throw a person overboard in the Alps if you pay him enough. Or, he'll rig a parachute for you and fly you right over that dead city so you can go exploring (but find your own way back).

Like every great aviator, though, he has a pretty big obstacle he must overcome before he finally arrives at the success he desires, and it's no physical mountain. It's booze. So when he's wining and dining with the women (and dandies) who want to hear his stories, he will proclaim the legendary pilots' feats as his own, to the laughter of the more learned skeptics at the party, who know the last name of those heroes certainly isn't Hickburn (or the last name Bran is using at the time).

Finally, the booze lets Bran loose his tongue as to his darker side: he's a BDSM'er. Leather, whips, cuffs, pain and pleasure, dominatrix-lover, yup, it's all there. Just no animals. That would be truly disgusting, and anyone who suggests such a thing he'd gladly throw overboard when his ship is steaming over the ocean. He's very careful to only have these parties in his skyship, and only with those who want to travel, and only if they are not aviators, too. (Wouldn't want someone throwing *him* overboard and stealing his ship!)

The only thing, he can't remember all the last names he's used, or where he's suspected of kidnapping or murder because his passengers went missing. But he has a lot of rich friends in those towns...and they just might hire him again if you're nosy.

DADDY LONGLEGS, MERCHANT

Personality Quick Look

Deportment

Hustle hustle make that money! No idle standing around. Time is money. What you want? I can get it. That? Oh, that will cost you extra...

Temperament

A true businessman never shows anger, except when someone mistreats his wares. And since his girls are his merchandise, his anger is quick and swift when it comes to these beauties.

Past Sins

He's had business towns where his services are illegal, so some constables...

Future Goals

Yeah, Mayor, some day. And perhaps he'll name the town Brothel.

Daddy Longlegs is a true merchant, not one of these charlatans that go from town to town to swindle people, and he will challenge anyone who claims otherwise (of course, he'll cheat in the duel, having one of his girls shoot you in the head just as you're about to turn around to shoot at him).

Daddy Longlegs, "DL" to his friends, has been known to travel from town to town, but only to those towns where he can ply his trades legally. He wants no part of incurring the wrath of any overzealous Constable; he's all too familiar with the stories about Bucketswill.

Of course, that's the official story. But DL deals more in the secrets of others, and his Ladies are quite adept at pumping their clients for information. Yes, his ladies act SO innocent, but they know exactly what the game is, and they know exactly how to win.

While his moniker seems cheeky or absurd to some, so long as his cover story is believed, there are those "off grid" who know better, and stand awed in his presence. Just like a spider, DL weaves his web, spinning it to catch his victims in a very methodical, meticulous, sometimes diabolical way. And there are those who hire him to do just that to their enemies.

His services are pricey, since he has an army to feed, and it's a price that no one ever fully pays off: as soon as someone hires him to weave a web, they also become cogs in a machine, cogs that might serve a needful purpose later on, in some unrelated plot, or conspiracy, against yet another victim.

Even the bum on the street, drunken and slothful, might owe DL a favor or three. If it could be said, DL is the Mayor of the underground, the off grid seedier civilization the town never admits to having.

That being said, he doesn't know everything. He doesn't know who The Clipper is, really, although he has his suspicions, and he has employed him/her on several occasions. He's also arranged things with Hickburn once or twice (in fact, he's the reason for Ms. Hurst's fifth husband's demise), so she'll be owing him a favor, too.

DL is not quick to collect favors, though, calling them in perhaps years later. Sometimes, people try not to pay. Well, DL has a solution for that, too. But you won't know what that solution is, or who delivers it, until the web closes over you, binding you to the fate DL has decreed for you, and you hang helplessly in the spider's embrace.

THE FABULOUS PYRO SISTERS

Personality Quick Look

Deportment

Smalls is the one who will serve you up for breakfast, naked, bound, gagged, helpless and begging. Talls is the one who will eat you for breakfast.

Temperament

Ready always to draw their weapons and shoot with no hesitation. Alert, wily, and smart, they know their shit.

Past Sins

Nothing anyone still living would dare tell. And they're very good at keeping their third sister from being discovered. (She usually plays the monster).

Future Goals

To find 3 hubbies who will keep their secret (and the money flowing in)...

Occasionally using fire against monsters that terrorize towns (and thereby destroying all evidence and leaving a charred animalistic husk-corpse to prove they got the monster), the Fabulous Pyro Sisters remain in popular demand!

The two of them are invited by unsuspecting Mayors who give in to the demands of their townsfolk fearful of their lives. At first, the signs will be barely noticeable: one of the livestock gets maimed or goes missing. Then more signs begin to instill fear as a cow or chicken gets viciously and bloodily killed. Perhaps then a sighting or two of a huge furry monster, perhaps chasing a child through the forest and she drops her carefully picked bouquet in terror.

Whatever, the case, the Fabulous Pyro Sisters will come to the aid of the suffering town, humbly charging a fee commensurate with the level of their services (up front, of course, with additional expenses tacked on for good measure as time goes on, and the monster hunt proves to exhaust their "resources.").

When they're not monster hunting or sleeping in the finest lodgings the town's money can afford, the sisters are on constant lookout for worthy men who might make suitable lifelong companions. Most, of course, are completely unworthy and not to be trusted. But eventually, they'll run across a man or three who know how to keep their secret, and perhaps even expand their monster-hunter capability.

Each of the sisters is a true skeptic when it comes to haunts or monsters of any type, and they'll first search out the true perpetrators by canvassing the entire town with investigative techniques that are far superior to all but the most aspiring constables.

Then, they'll simply blackmail the perpetrators, or actually go into business with them for purposes of fleecing the town. In the latter case, they'll consider whether the perps could make good husbands (if they're male), and if not, will find some way to end their business relationship.

Thus far, the sisters have not run up against a real monster, and while they know this might be a possibility, feel they are probably up to the challenge, since they are very adept at hand to hand combat and using their weapons (and explosives).

Finally, the third sister, Balls, is the fiercest of the three, and if you piss her off or otherwise try to compromise their gig, you'll never see her coming...

PUG MALLORY, FIXER

How can you take someone who's name is Pug seriously? I mean, hey, Pug, you're really smart, I think I'll take your advice. Really? Come on. If his name was Elliot, or Alexander, certainly Maximillian. But Pug? Yeah right. Go get me a beer, Pug.

But it's a simple fact that Pug knows everyone and all their secrets. Everyone knows he's harmless, so no one feels like they have to suspect him of anything. He's the unseen servant who's allowed to pour the ale while the big men (or big women) talk about their shady dealings.

Perhaps this is all fine to Pug, who, in fact, might just be the idiot everyone thinks him to be. Or, it might just be an act he puts on while hiding the genius that he truly is. In fact, when used once by Daddy Longlegs, he fucked everything up royally, so he feels confident DL will never come knocking again or otherwise call in any other favors.

The funny thing is, though, that as much as people see him as accident-prone, he is one of the luckiest bastards alive. Again, is it just luck? Or does he plan things to go exactly, haphazardly, the way he wants them to? Only he can tell you that, as no one has caught him arranging things, nor does he work well with others. Heck, "work" isn't even in his vocabulary. But he's like a hyperventilating puppy dog, always there with ideas, always talking about everything he's heard, whether it's true or not.

He wants only to be your friend. And he's loyal to a fault, until his ADD-ADHD kicks in and he drops you like a hot potato for the next thing that caught his attention.

People have tried to punish him for being him, but he just thinks it's game, even when they're throwing deadly knives at his head to teach him a lesson or because someone stole their dartboard.

He's vehement, though, that there are sinister entities always trying to read his mind or make suggestions, and that's why he is seldom found without his mind-shielding hat. Often, he will make your acquaintance by suggesting you get a mind-shielding hat of your own, and he has an extra one to sell you, ahh, if you treat him like a friend, he'll just give it to you for free.

While no one except him knows whether he's a genius or an idiot, one thing is certain, although he might not remember: he was accidentally standing on a minor plexus during the EMP war, and although he wasn't absorbed into the Overmind, he is sensitive to some of the Cabal's broadcasts.

SIGMOND THE HEAVY EXPLORER

Need an armor piercing bullet for that rifle your grandfather gave you? Or perhaps an armored vest from the Old World because you're about to make your move for Mayor? No worries, Sigmond knows exactly where to look for such things, and for a modest fee, he'll brave the radioactive ruins to go looking for it.

What he would never tell you, though, is that he would have done it for free. He loves exploring, loves the challenge of surviving against all odds, and while he should have died long ago from "The Sickness" (radiation sickness that explorers often die from), he's been lucky so far. Or maybe, he's especially immune because he's just a strong, healthy man.

Indeed, he could probably outrun a deer, he's so fit.

And strong. Neither horses nor vehicles are able to navigate the dangerous ruins he goes to. He often must step over rebar and large, heavy cement fragments, steel beams, glass shards, and hard sharp things. He must carry his tools in, and then his tools and treasure out. Sometimes, he goes under the ruins into what once were subways or sewer systems — dozens and dozens of miles of twisting, turning tunnels in some Dead Cities that literally were that big!

He's gotten lost many times, but he had the tools to survive. Unbeknownst to others, he has several artifacts he's found and kept to himself, and his water-making machine is not the least of them.

Occasionally, bandits lie in wait for him, to try to snatch up what he risked his life to retrieve. That's why he never takes the same road twice, and if he gets jumped, he has a couple of artifacts for that, too. And he won't risk being merciful. His rep can't handle it. Bandits know that if they fuck with him, they die. He's let a couple of the cowards go just to spread the word, laughing loudly as they fled for their lives into the dark.

He's become a legend to many, that way, but few would know his face. So he could be sitting having a beer in some tavern and no one would be the wiser, no one would suspect that he was Sigmond the Heavy. He certainly likes his solitude, and the freedom his lifestyle affords.

But he's getting older, and he knows ruin-running is for the young and strong. He has stashes of goodies all over the place, some buried, some in houses he owns in several towns. Perhaps it's time he starts his own Explorer's Guild. If he ever finds a worthy protegé, he just might.

HERSCHEL CLAYTON IVERSON

A true scholar at heart, Herschel (he prefers "Clay") Iverson dabbles in all manner of inventions and steam power, prizing Old World books more highly than the love of women (though he'll relish their attentions until he's bored), so long as those books show him centrifuges, electricity, blueprints for machines, and also speak about the Venturi principle.

He's the one who's going to discover how to isolate the invisible aether and to use it to launch his inventions into the future. Time travel is not beyond his ability, and once he reads the right book, once he obtains the right material, yea, once he conducts the right (human) experiment, he'll discover those precious secrets that elude lesser minds.

He often receives — and ignores — High Society invites. His studies and lab work are ever so much more important than slinging insults at a bunch of fools. But sometimes, he has to play the part of a gentleman in their circles because he has to: his lab has astronomical costs: chemicals must be bought, explorers must be paid, merchants and chemists are often also on his payroll, and when he realizes he hasn't eaten in about four days, he'll see that his money jar is empty and show up unannounced at one of the High Society functions.

They of course know what he's there for: their money, and so they make him earn it. At first, he is loathe to share his progress with minds that could not possibly understand the intricacies of his work, but after a drink or two, and spurred on by all the praise he's received for the various inventions he's already published, he fits right into the role they want from him: Philosopher, but he prefers the exalted title, "Master Inventor."

Is this possible? Is that possible? Have you ever heard of this type of machine? Is aether here or is it just in the heavens? Time travel, your thoughts? Space travel, your thoughts?

And so the night goes, and he talks nonstop, but he's very careful to never divulge his current project or anything he's discovered that other inventors might use to surpass his progress. And he would think that they could be trying to break into his windowless lab/shop, were it not for the fifteen locks he had on the one door and the three booby-traps he left for them.

Clay enjoys the admiration, support, and protection of the High Society clique as well as the respect of the lowly cogs of the town. Indeed, his only enemies are those who would steal his ideas or otherwise hamper his progress. And those enemies deserve what they have coming to them.

THE WANDERER

While there are several dozens of original Overmind Cabal members who were created and mutated during the EMP/Nuke World War III as they centered (meditated trying to receive MTAP) on leylines and places where leylines intersected (plexuses), none is so terrorizing as the one people call "The Wanderer." Of course, they only whisper the name. No need for the boogie man to think you're calling him…

The Wanderer is rumored to be a powerful Immortal who has magical powers. He is every child's nightmare and how every mother keeps her children in line: don't be a bad kid or else The Wanderer will eat you!

If the Overmind can be said to have a hierarchy, The Wanderer would be pretty high up. Some of the Ancient Races believe that The Wanderer is who was once known as Vibius Juventius Graius Draconis, or He Who Roams, and that's why he only destroys those who attack him, because he's really a benevolent (though changed) being.

Others, and they cannot be convinced otherwise, claim that The Wanderer is a Marune, or worse yet, He Who Stands Alone, who, knowing that something weird would happen during the EMP war, purposely stood on a major plexus so that a change could happen and he could then use magic.

Still others claim that he's just a normal man in a suit with a light and fog machine, trying to make a name for himself.

Whatever the truth is, it remains to be proven, as most who have met the creature have not lived to tell about it, and if they have, their memories are foggy or the stories are just so outrageous as to make others believe they've gone nuts.

You, Storyteller, might to well to remember that the Cabal don't have to be this mysterious or famous. Perhaps Pug Mallory is a Cabal, and just doesn't know it yet. And they could be anyone, anywhere: steamboat captains, aviators, inventors, and they don't have to shoot out magical rays just to be Cabal.

But one thing's for certain, the Overmind hasn't deemed it time to walk about openly as anything other than strange, introverted loners, observing potential victims from afar while the Overmind studies them. When it is time, the Overmind will give the order, and human subjects will be taken for experiments. Until then, the Cabal must blend in or remain far away from the possibility of being discovered as part of the Overmind collective. In that sense, The Wanderer is an exception; could he/she/it be the core of the Overmind?

MINOR PERSONALITIES

If you've played Immortal Empires in the original setting of the 6th and 7th Age (as explained in the two core rulebooks), you know that just because one of your Storyteller characters is a "Minor" Personality does not mean they will stay a minor personality, nor does it mean they are unimportant to the story. It may well be that the Minor Personality becomes Mayor (or Emperor!) with proper interaction and support from your players.

Take, for instance, Dr. Ives Perrywrinkle (pictured above). Yes, he carries a sidearm (but who doesn't in these dangerous times?), yes he wears what could be a High Society hat, as he's well enough to do with in-house machines (like the telephone and electric heater behind him), but he's just one of many more wealthy minor characters who populate the town. The players might never meet him.

Or, he might become central to their story. Perhaps they've broken the law and are hunted and need a facelift (actually a face-change!), or perhaps one of them was so disrespectful to

him as to stirred his ire and now he seeks to skin them alive, because well, you know, he's mental like that.

Suddenly, Dr. Ives will have become a Major Personality without anyone (even you, Storyteller) having planned it. It just all depends on where the story goes, and since you are only one person of several interacting with the world, maybe even you will be surprised.

In the following chart, we've outlined 60 minor personalities who may or may not know each other, who may or may not be in the same town, etc. That's all for you to decide. But we have helped by giving you their names, ages, vocations, whether or not they have friends (and if they're powerful), their illicit reputation IF they deal in off grid matters, and a short list of their traits, flaws, sins, and goals.

It's up to you to fill out the rest. Some of them could be Immortal Ancient Races hiding in plain sight; others could be just normal ZERO ORank nobodies living their lives as best they can. Either way, they're bound to make Steampunk fun.

	NAME	AGE	VOCATION	FRIENDS	ILL REP	TRAIT FLAW SIN GOAL
1	**Ives Perrywrinkle**	40	Preacher - Surgeon	Few	Great Plastic Surgeon	Patient, soft-spoken, but hides a dark side: will skin you alive if you piss him off
2	**Megaria Riverscourt**	75	Aristocrat	Many High Society	No	Second runner up for control of the town gossip, matriarch, grandmotherly, wise!
3	**Thorne Longfellow**	49	Corner Store Merchant	Many Merchants	Maybe	Happy to please, meticulous on how much people owe him, coin is king
4	**Midas Earlfring**	33	Charlatan	His wife, Mida	Con Artist	Runs 2-man cons with his wife. Occasionally his daughter & son help the con
5	**Carlton Muskerton**	22	Constable	Many young	No	Having been a constable from 16, he's fiercely loyal, wants to be Chief constable
6	**Phillipp Shornstave**	17	Explorer wannabe	Many young	No	Currently a constable, he wants nothing more than to go exploring. Hates being trapped as a constable. Slightly immature
7	**Marge Upticutt**	55	Aristocrat	Few High Society	Butcher of Hale Street	Loves her little dog. Is thought to have murdered Hale cogs when they "stole" it
8	**Beverly Sumpfork**	46	House Maid	Many in low places	No	The lowly maid...but ruler of the household, she's leader of the cog rumor mill in the town, giving gossip but wisely able to manipulate what she gossips for her own gain; could lead a cog rebellion...
9	**Thatch Overbridge**	30	Street Ruffian	Few	Merc 4 Hire	A dumbass, but smart enough to know he is, he's good muscle if anyone needs it
0	**Hatch Overbridge**	30	Street Ruffian	Very few	Merc 4 Hire	A dumbass, but too dumb to know his twin "bro" is too; stronger, dumber than Thatch; has a weakness for pretty rodents
1	**Magnolia Sifter**	69	High Society wannabe, constable wife	Very few	No	Nag, overly suspicious of everyone and runs to report "crimes" to her husband
2	**Katelind Nightingowl**	68	Town Baker	Many	Messenger Service	Obese fails to convey how big Katelind is (the kids call her NightingCow). But she can get a message to anyone Off Grid; just ask for special icing on your cupcake.
3	**Bryan S. Hurdling**	50	Inventor	None	The Anvil	Works on military-style inventions, fulfills illicit Off Grid weapon requests
4	**Cornelia Fastspring**	27	Hooker	Many low-lifes	DL's Right Hand	Always on the lookout for new recruits, runs a tight, loyal ship, likes to punish
5	**Halper Min**	63	Chemist	Some High Society	No	Runs the town apothecary, is searching for a cure all, and uses volunteers for tests
6	**Furia Nuvola**	35	Aristocrat	Few High Society	Lady Rose	Leader of the shady Lady Roses, a network of gossips who regularly sip poison to build their resistance: their kiss kills.
7	**Drago Africanus**	73	Aristocrat	Few High Society	The Dark Sage	Advice as dark and evil as his coal black skin, seems to know everything! A Master Scholar... at last (hint hint).
8	**Lip Beagler**	54	Aristocrat	Many High Society	No	Having "quarterback" popularity among High Society, smart, tough, insightful
9	**Putsy Orbrion**	59	Aristocrat	Cogs only	Maybe	Completely disdained by High Society but tolerated because he's rich, secretive
0	**Jackson McKindleson**	20	Aristocrat	Few other young High Society	No	Envied by others for being the current favorite of the doting Mayor, vehemently denies any sexual relations with mayor, but enjoys Mayor's protection

STEAMTOWN CANVASSED DOSSIER --- PAGE 1 OF 3

(S-RD)

RESTRICTED DATA
SECRET

	NAME	AGE	VOCATION	FRIENDS	ILL REP	TRAIT FLAW SIN GOAL
1	**Norm Rancher**	48	Gunslinger Preacher	No	the "Monk"	Lives outside of town on a small cattle ranch, rights wrongs, prattles on about treating the cogs right, especially Karla…
2	**Lump Olaffson**	30	Out of work Explorer, boozing it up	No, just passing through	Maybe	Lazy until he gets in the mood, spends all his money on booze, will scavenge 4 pay
3	**Mark Swigwell**	44	Submergible Captain	Only his 5 member crew	Maybe	He's ready to explore under the ocean, as soon as he gets that one part he needs to fix his submersible (of course there is no part he needs, but he wants to get paid!)
4	**Karla Matthewsring**	37	Barmaid	Norm	No	Slightly attractive, I can handle myself, thank you, swarthy barmaid, but allows Norm to dote so long as he buys a drink
5	**Felix Ablerwockey**	19	Preacher	Many	No	Extremely handsome, ladies & girls dream about him, he's out to make a better world for everyone, even if that means making it worse for some, shaming their privilege (but still High Society women can't help themselves, lusting after him)
6	**Morgan Jiltz**	16	Teacher Apprentice	Many children	No	Popular, pretty and smart girl just out of school herself, is the only "kid" bullies never bully, plans to be an aviator soon
7	**Greta O'Connors**	32	Explorer	Some Cogs	No	While not as good as other explorers she knows how to survive; charges less than others
8	**Butch "Eyeball" Herv**	59	Dentist	His wife, Ellie	Maybe	Does the painful dentist work, named for his mechanical eyeball that snakes into people's mouths while he's looking for cavities
9	**Lesch Favorton**	33	Balloonist	Many	Maybe	Not quite an aviator, dealing solely in humongous basket-lofting balloons, gives free rides, but never knows where he will end up
0	**Dan Widdlecock**	72	Aristocrat	Few	25 Years ago: "the Jackal"	Mean as they come, appears to find dogs AND Cogs loathsome, Won't talk about his illicit career off grid when he was merc 4 hire, claiming that he reformed after a long stretch in Miregold, Steamtown's Workhouse.
1	**Earl Rochessler, III**	55	Aristocrat	No	No	Overly proud of Aristocrat status, cannot fathom that his class would tolerate criminals, cannot stand Widdlecock, but fears him
2	**Faye Lovecrest**	23	Printing Press / Journalist	Several Cogs	No	Pretty and good-mannered for a lowly Cog, she will end up marrying into the Aristocracy
3	**Burk Donaldson**	52	Aristocracy / Owns town Press	Several Cogs	No	Good-natured but often puts Aristocracy dirty laundry in the town paper, no secret is safe
4	**Angela Frothbirth**	41	Nursemaid / Nanny	Many High Society	Maybe	The hand that rocks the cradle, she has many High Society children who love her…
5	**Hauser Riechestein**	45	Blacksmith	Cogs	Maybe	Very strong, keeps to his own family, isn't afraid to work on Skydrop Steel, seems overly interested in shackles (displays them in shop)
6	**Carolinia Fallstaff**	60	Aristocrat	Her Lady Butterflies	Maybe	Running her own gossip-group of ladies, she cannot stand Nuvola, always tries to upstage
7	**Hank "Leech" Beecher**	14	Jules Blackleaf's beefy sidekick	Jules Blackleaf	Probably Soon	Sneaks booze, cornfed (looks like adult), borrows but never returns item, brat-bully
8	**Destiny Blackleaf**	39	Aristocrat	Some	Maybe	Possibly a man (crossdresser), flirts openly with Mayor in front of husband Piers
9	**Piers Blackleaf**	43	Aristocrat	No	No	Seems powerless to stop his wife from cuckolding him, could be a time bomb waiting to….
0	**Jules Blackleaf**	12	School Bully	Hank Beecher	Probably Soon	Thief, rebel, embarrassment to parents, keeps other kids terrified of him; criticizes Mayor

STEAMTOWN CANVASSED DOSSIER --- PAGE 2 OF 3

(S-RD)
RESTRICTED DATA
SECRET

	NAME	AGE	VOCATION	FRIENDS	ILL REP	TRAIT FLAW SIN GOAL
1	**Hathaway Fezzler**	26	Aristocrat	High Society Youth Clique	Unknown	Apparently the leader of the H.S. Youth Clique, loves debating, fine drink, and appears to be in line for Mayor someday, disdained by Mayor
2	**Brock Morrisonson**	29	Aristocrat	High Society Youth Clique	Unknown	Very uppity, snobbish, acts over-intelligent, excuses himself with windy sophistic "intellectual" arguments when he is found to err
3	**Elias Bonapartez**	23	Aristocrat	High Society Youth Clique	Unknown	A foreigner, apparently an orphan, who, because of his true intellect has been accepted into the clique, a favorite of Hathaway, his expenses are usually paid by him
4	**Fredrick Anderly**	22	Aristocrat	High Society Youth Clique	Unknown	Hathaway's best pal, the two of them often run cons on the rest of the group (all in fun, of course), is suspicious of and unfriendly to those who are not in the clique
5	**Ketch Harold**	25	Aristocrat	High Society Youth Clique	Unknown	The instigator, will pose questions so as to pit one member of the group against another, has done this to cogs as well, for fun...
6	**Dawn Millhouse**	25	Aristocrat	High Society Youth Clique	Unknown	Completely head over heels in love with Hathaway, has spoken openly that she would kill for him, jealous of Fredrick's influence over Hathaway, but tries to keep her cool
7	**Isabella Cortessa**	22	Aristocrat	High Society Youth Clique	Unknown	Secretly loves Hathaway, but afraid of Dawn, relegates herself to act interested in Fredrick
8	**Michael Llewellyn**	30	Aristocrat	High Society Youth Clique	Unknown	Probably the most intellectual of the group, sincerely tries to explain why others (especially Brock) are wrong, seems ashamed of the clique's reputation when asked in public
9	**Madge Burner**	27	Aristocrat	High Society Youth Clique	Unknown	Smoker, drinker, not afraid to scuff it out with anyone, even Hathaway, might be lesbian
0	**Donny Figuroa, Esq.**	26	Aristocrat / Lawyer	High Society Youth Clique	Unknown	Knows the town's laws inside and out, and for that reason how to bend them, bookworm
1	**Georg Shaletown**	19	Cog	Cog Youth Clique	Unknown	Definitely the leader of the Cog youths, Georg is the son of Bjorn, Steamtown's sanitation chief, entertains Cog youth with grand stories of what he finds in Aristocrat garbage and in the sewers, completely in love with Hannah
2	**Buck "Wildskin" Hure**	21	Cog	Cog Youth Clique	Unknown	Used to be Georg's best friend until Hannah, now hunts alone, unafraid of anyone
3	**Fiona MacEntire**	17	Cog	Cog Youth Clique	Unknown	In between laundry-maid duties, Fiona tries to catch a glimpse of Buck shirtless...
4	**Cassiopoeia Bumsgart**	23	Cog	Cog Youth Clique	Unknown	Rueful that she is not High Society privileged, can say nothing good about them, plots
5	**Hillary Shortshaft**	25	Cog	Cog Youth Clique	Unknown	Cassiopoeia's counterpart often in trouble with High Society for doing what Cassy wishes...
6	**Stirewalt Greaves**	29	Cog	Cog Youth Clique	Unknown	Apprenticed to Hauser, has the largest muscle, but is completely unaware of Hannah's ogling
7	**Max Hilderscout**	24	Cog	Cog Youth Clique	Unknown	Plays the gofer for Clay Iverson, as such he has many stories of what he catches glimpses of
8	**Yennifer Laffton**	21	Cog	Cog Youth Clique	Unknown	A mute, probably the most ignored young woman in all the town, but wooed by Buck
9	**Grieg Borscht**	24	Cog	Cog Youth Clique	Unknown	The smartass of the group, has a quip for everything, has spent time in the workhouse
0	**Hannah Silverscourt**	20	Cog	Cog Youth Clique	Unknown	Long hair, graceful, spends time singing while fulfilling her knitting duties, intelligent

WITHOUT EXCEPTION, NON-INFLUENTIAL PERSONALITIES ARE NOT INCLUDED IN THIS SUMMARY

STEAMTOWN CANVASSED DOSSIER --- PAGE 3 OF 3

RESTRICTED DATA
SECRET
(S-RD)

MONSTERS

Really? Monsters in Steampunk? Well, of course! Even True Steampunk has abominations, results of failed experiments, that populate the cemeteries, the waters of the deep, and yes, even the skies.

Immortal Empires, as you may know, takes it a step further: the true monster is that villain who's sending the abominations after you, and could be the Mayor, the Constable, or even Madam Sylvia Hurst (but she prefers to do the job herself, normally). After all, we're dealing with high level stuff here, immortals, actually, and our designs, machinations, if you will, aspire to more lofty places than to eradicate a silly goblin lair (okay, we admit, perhaps that's an unfair shot at other games, but this is one of the reasons we like Immortal Empires so much: it's ever so much more complex and involved. Just when you think you got the "monster's" stereotype figured out, it changes, because it was just the symptom, an extension, of the real enemy who actually uses their intellect against you!).

Steampunk adds all sorts of potential symptoms and classes of so-called monster. There are mechanical spies dressed as insects that might be carrying a syringe of poison your way. There are mechanical beasts set as guards around labs (and underwater-based hideouts). There are mangy hybrid animals terrorizing the towns, no doubt results of radiation-related degeneration. There might even be vampires or ghosts (or just the high society Madam who wishes she were, like Ms. Báthory...).

And just because it's Immortal Empires, let's throw in things even more dangerous, to challenge whatever Immortal Players have survived to this Age. Marune Minions, yea, even Marunes themselves, still walk the earth in search of those who would Bargain for immediate power instead of work hard to earn it. And let's not forget the Cabal and the wrench they might throw into the Marunes' plans.

Whatever your fancy, there are plenty of monstrosities you can insert into your Story to give your players a good challenge, but we humbly ask, that you honor the eclectic sophistication of Immortal Empires: the real monster should be a Personality.

Who would be able to forget that there might be vampires in your Steampunk Story? Not us. But we might add here that True Steampunk avoids the supernatural, and we respect that completely! We include the supernatural here only for Enhanced Steampunk stories.

Now let's think about this. Not every person who thinks they must survive on blood is a real vampire; they could just be completely insane or just downright cruel: Vlad the Impaler, Countess Elizabeth Báthory de Ecsed, Rasputin (who enjoyed humiliating High Society women), H.H. Holmes, Jack the Ripper, just to name a few.

But then again, there really might be some vampires walking around Steampunk, and that would explain why some people only come out at night, blaming their aversion to the bright sunlight on absinthe, of course.

Whatever your Story, you need not stick to just one popular legend (Dracula), but you might include other lesser known legends: the ghouls of Arabia, the Babylonian tales of the Lilitu, the Strix of Ancient Rome, the Empusa and Lamia of the Greeks, the Vetalas of India, the Alukah of the Hebrews, the Revenants of Medieval Europe, the Vampires of Voltaire, the baby-sucking Shtriga of Albania, the Draugar of Iceland, the Moroi of Romania, the Bruxas of Portugal, the Morana of Croatia, the Guaxa of Hispania, the iron-toothed asanbosam of West Africa, the ramanga of Madagascar, and the list goes on.

Suffice it to say that there are myriad storylines and different legends you can include if you choose to adulterate Steampunk with the supernatural...and then there's werewolves.

Yes, the High Society elites are at it again, trying to scare each other into believing that there are ghosts.

And maybe there are, in Steampunk, at least. Could be a knocking sound, maybe a rattle, or a full-on sighting of the skeletal anomaly floating down the stairs as in the illustration to the left.

Of course, it could also be an Inventor who, with or without aether (or perhaps an ancient artifact with the ability to do Glimmerings), who's projecting the smoke and mirrors image just to fool you into hiring his friend Bork the Monster Hunter so they can split the proceeds with each other.

In any case, Steampunk ghosts are more than just a bed sheet rising up from the bed. There's usually a very rational explanation for them, if you aren't too scared to find out.

While The Wanderer certainly deserves an exalted seat at the Major Personalities roundtable, there are other Cabal no less intimidating who can cause all manner of mayhem in your Story.

You'll do well to remember that the Ancient Races will have a much better idea of and defense against the Overmind legion, probably viewing them in much the same light as they view Marunes and Marune Minions. Much better, that is, than the carefree High Society and hard-working Cog classes of Newborn that vast and large inhabit what's left of the surviving world. In fact, it could be said that while the Newborn are trying to identify and eliminate any and all Ancient Races, the Ancient Races are trying to identify and eliminate all of the Cabal. Better that than becoming enslaved by the Overmind!

As for "powers" of the Cabal, they would probably have magical ability much like the Ancient Races, but as MTAP is extremely scarce, they wouldn't be using it either, except in rare cases the Overmind deems necessary. So, the Overmind would prioritize machine development and technological research with a view towards the future domination of all species.

In fact, it may well be that the Cabal is behind the gadgets gone wild (monster below), having made them as experiments to how they might integrate with or obey the Overmind. In that case, there would be one, two, or more Cabal in the area just trying to observe how their creation terrorizes the citizens of Steampunk. If a Cabal is spotted, they might just run away; then again, they might join in the terror!

Occasionally, there really are monsters, these in the form of Inventor gadgets gone wild. They could be any size, enjoy steam power or wind-up spring power as seen in the illustration, and literally have some type of "mind" of their own, especially if the Inventor experimented with some type of artifact s/he got from another millennium.

Not all animal designs merely imitate the animal. For example, instead of just teeth and the ability to run fast, this design has a tail that can perform a serious, metal-lashing attack. Perhaps also, there's a pistol in the animal's maw.

You can get really creative with inventions gone wild, if you care to, including, if your Story is up to it, aether-based artificial intelligence. After all, Cyber Age Hostilities are just around the corner.

Some monsters are sheeple in wolves clothing. Literally, or in the case to the left, people in feathers trying to play the part of a wicked monster stalking the only the High Society members at night. What better way to make the arrogant elite afraid of the lowly Cogs who wait on them hand and foot, night and day?

These types of monsters might have an artifact or two to help them maintain the mystery about them as well as make them dangerous (or super-human). They could be anyone, maybe even "Balls" from the Fabulous Pyro Sisters.

Then again, these could be Ancient Race Immortals fed up with having to remain in hiding. Much better to let the Newborn fear them and eliminate them one by one until such a time as the Ancients can show their faces again.

Then there are the Marune Minions, people who seem normal in every way, but who have made a deal with He Who Stands Alone or any of Those Who Run Together. The Marunes' ultimate goal is to deprive the Presidium of their Star Legions when they return, and the Marune's Minions have no choice but to carry out directive they receive from their masters using special gifts they've bargained for.

Often, that means death and destruction for others, while the Minion slowly goes insane, having given in completely to the special type of Corruption that flows to them from their particular dark master.

But some of the Minions get lucky, having amassed power enough without going nuts so as to receive the coveted promotion to Marune Consort. Even Immortals fears these...

Let's not forget the sea creatures! Inventors love to make stuff for the Greater World of ocean and depth. Maybe they're searching for sunken treasure; maybe they're searching for the fabled Atlantis.

And maybe the reason some of their mechanical monsters don't come back is because there are real monsters — the Kraken, the Leviathan, Charybdis, among others — that can really ruin a submersible Captain's day.

Remember that the Newborn were just beginning to explore the seas before the EMP/Nuke catastrophe plunged the world back a hundred years. So it is relatively a New Frontier, still, in the Steampunk era, with many unknowns, including mutated abominations resulting from the fallout, not to forget that there are Atlantean Cabal down here too.

STEAMPUNK STORIES

PART NINE

In the Immortal Empires game world, Steampunk has its own place, but we strive to have it keep the unique flavor and wealth that makes Immortal Empires stand above other game worlds out there. In this section we'll explain how to keep your Story true to the Immortal Empires vision.

IMMORTAL EMPIRES IS DIFFERENT...

From the beginning, Immortal Empires has its own world, fantastical history, and twists, not to mention a level of believable realism woven into the storytelling. But that is not what sets it apart (and above) other fantasy games.

We have always wanted Immortal Empires to be a game full of *real* knowledge that people could learn and use in their real lives, whether it be historical races and customs, ancient tools and Personalities, Latin, or an expanded English vocabulary, simple math and physics applications, how to act convincingly, an enhanced ability to solve problems, military strategy, or the fine art of Storytelling itself.

Our version of Steampunk, though perhaps purely fictional, still should be rooted in what scientifically *could* be. We make mention herein of High Society members debating each other with philosophical ideas, and that's how we'd like you to enjoy this rules expansion, too. Just *what* could be possible if the world was set back a hundred or so years? Will your players join you in that belief or think you're just a dreamer? Will they put your ideas for Steampunk to the test? Will they challenge you with their own ideas and surprise you???

Just like our Imperial and Medieval Ages are not at all about killing goblins with a watered-down role-playing system (and a spear and magic helmet), so, too, our Steampunk expansion isn't merely about pipes and steam and clockwork.

In both cases, the Story is really about the people: Personalities and Players alike and what great, heroic lives they're able to live in the game world.

How will your players get to the top? Will they scheme and lie (and murder) their way? Or will they become so beloved by the Cogs so as to force their way into High Society? Either way involves manipulation. Either way involves preparation. And each path will have those who try to stop them.

On Grid, Off Grid, attacks from all sides, under the ocean, in the sky, Steampunk has a lot to offer, including the unique additions of Marunes and Ancient Races and the Overmind all competing to place themselves in *your* Official Story.

It, ultimately, is up to you and your players to decide!

Steamtown

We've been a little cheeky here, naming our town Steamtown, but it can be any name you want. The Personalities in the Bestiarium can all be in the same town (that's how we've written it, actually) or they can be from several towns. This booklet is just to get you started. You are more than welcome to make a whole bunch of towns, ruined radioactive cities, and machines to explore everything.

Perhaps your players might even discovered the long lost Atlantis! Perhaps the Atlanteans there won't kill them... Or perhaps the Atlanteans are extinct. Only you know!

Cyber Age Hostilities

Steampunk in Immortal Empires is also different because the Official Story is progressing along the time continuum towards the Cyber Age, a dark robotic world where corporations, not governments, are the new masters and protectors of the people.

People in this age are on the verge of losing their humanity and their trust of their fellow man. We envision it to be something like Jesus Christ prophesized: "Because iniquity shall abound, the love of many shall wax cold" (KJV, Matthew 24:12).

Cyber Age Hostilities is an age where people have replaced "absolute" or "universal" morality (where evil towards others is bad because everyone agrees it is bad) with "relative" morality ("I can do what you think is evil because I don't think it's evil"). The chaos that results from relativism is held in check only by the iron fists of Corporations that have the financial means to enforce whatever laws they deem appropriate for their sphere of influence, and it may well come down to: "If you murder, you die, unless you murder someone from our rival Corporation, then we'll give you a promotion..."

So, with the descent of mankind into the dark future of Cyber Age in mind, you should make Steampunk ever more joyous and fantastic, phenomenal, while giving hints occasionally of darker times to come, even while technology advances.

World Considerations

Remember that the EMP/Nuke war was a world-wide catastrophe. That means that cities and cultures, Rus, Oshekoga, Osh, Lahavia, Rotha, Astoria, Arkadia, Africa, Ammoria, and even the Atlanteans' cities (Neptunis, Atlantis), were all affected, if not nearly destroyed with heavy damage.

To run Steampunk in a different culture might be a challenge for you but should prove to be very rewarding for you and the players. How would those cultures choose to rebuild? Would they bring back feudal ways? Would they turn to Emperors? or Warlords?

Whatever your setting, the same Steampunk nostalgia and pre-industrial steam powered technology applies. It's just that people of different cultures might have different taboos and legends (just check back to the Monsters section about the vampires, for example). And the last thing: Please tell us your expanded world ideas on ImmortalEmpires.com!

Final Thoughts

We sincerely hope that you enjoy this rules expansion and consider it to be a great addition to your Immortal Empires story. I must confess that Steampunk wasn't a thing we were going to incorporate, but our team, now that the book is done, is so glad that we did.

To you Steampunk enthusiasts out there, Thank You! We had fun reading your blogs and viewing your art. We can imagine you getting dressed in your favorite Steampunk costumes just to get together for game night! We hope you choose Immortal Empires for your go-to game system. We also hope that you expand this little booklet to a great community that answers your demands and fills in area we've been found by you to be lacking.

Even if Steampunk isn't your thing, we hope that the special spin Immortal Empires puts on it makes it an acceptable, if not welcome, addition to your Official Story. Game on, Storytellers!

High Society

Appendix B: Bonus Content
Cyber Systems Hostilities: BETA

As a special thank you for buying this Rules Expansion, we've included our Beta notes on Cyber Systems Hostilities; just in case your Players figure out how to Time Travel to the future. We've also included the Cyber Age Character Records for you just in case that happens! Enjoy.

CYBER SYSTEMS HOSTILITIES ENVIRONMENT

Due to the technological achievements of the industrial age during previous Age (Dead World), magic has been relegated to a myth by the masses (even some wayward Ancient Race individuals attribute their magical phenomenon they accidentally use as LUCK or WEIRD SHIT that just happened because they were high on drugs at the time). But the Ancient Races who have kept their legacy through the Ages still have magic, but guard it jealously because of how slowly it replenishes (1 MTAP per year at the outset of the Cyber Age).

The Cyber Age technically begins with the discovery the first computer when governments still rule (lots of intrigue here as agents of all governments engage in national and corporate espionage as they set the stage for the Surveillance State(s)), but it doesn't come of age until the discovery of nanotechnology and picotechnology (when things really take off! ---heading towards the Galactic Age).

At the arrival of nanotechnology, Corporations begin to rule, while governments attempt to limit them (via anti-trust break ups, etc.). But as the corporations continue to grow in wealth (Apple, say, which even in our own reality has become the first TRILLION dollar company), they out step the capabilities of the governments and easily place their own Manchurian candidates in positions of power such that the governments are no longer autonomous but controlled by the powerful corporations. As such, governments are proxies of Corporate power.

This scenario matures as picotechnology makes biotech feasible, and the population growth of genetically enhanced humans, further enhanced with biotech outpaces the production of robots (which by now have evolved into androids that are nearly identical to humans (and which can only be distinguished by their innards).

As a result, the Ancient Races no longer need keep using their precious magic to remain hidden (Shapeshifted as Newborn races). The can just claim they are genetically enhanced humans. They might even have fake "biotech" that makes certain magical abilities possible (like innate Traits such as Third Eye which allows them to see magic (and makes their eyes have silver flakes floating in them). The Ancient Race immortals that have survived to this Age easily position themselves to be leaders of the New World Order (Corporations). And the old rivalries of the Ancient Houses re-emerge as they do so (which

could explain why Corporations arrange wars against other Corporations, even if they are not in competition for the same product sales).

As all technology is largely dependent on ELECTRICITY, industry has largely shifted to various (and cheapest) ways of creating a steady source of electricity (and perhaps harnessing electricity from storms that are so often man-made as to give the world a very dark and gloomy atmosphere (except of course, for those storm-free havens only the rich can afford)).

Money will have all been converted to Crypto Currency credits, with a very secret Elite Crypto Currency Available to only the ultra powerful. Only the Elite Crypto Currency is backed by actual value of assets (gold, diamonds, crops, guns, military engines, atomic/nuclear arsenals -- and each ECC unit comes with a designator to show what the Credit actually is: ECC-nuc might mean nuclear warhead; 3 ECC-nuc might mean 3 of them. Hence the masses are fooled into trading credits of no value whatsoever, but their belief that they are worth something is all that matters. Meanwhile, the ultra elites are actually trading powerful items of value for other powerful items or favors. The ECC will be SCI-TopSecret info, and any non-elite that finds out about it will necessarily be targeted for termination (OR invited to become an Ultra Elite, depending on their status).

All continents of the world are discovered and populated. All current nations can be represented if you want, including the U.S., Mexico, etc., but need not be the same in power as they are in our reality. Each government will either be struggling to maintain its independence from the ruling corporations or will be slaves to the ruling corporations. Checkpoints no longer check for citizenship but for corporate affiliation.

NAMING/ABBREVIATION CONVENTIONS

Legacy Weapons. Workmanship rating: example: L20 for a flintlock for ideal Legacy weapon workmanship 20, but that (and ammo) will degrade over time unless kept up. So a .45 well kept, could still have a L70. (a 71% roll means a misfire).

MicroTech: (Wm85 where 85 is the lowest Workmanship rating % for this tech). This technology is the beginning of advanced technology and is not as powerful as that which comes later (Terminator 1 vs. T2). MicroTech can only develop items and can not merge with biology directly, but can be used by humans: laser guns, laser cannon, sonic pulse weapons, microwave machines/weapons, etc. The abilities of MicroTech should be akin to the limitations Lesser Magic has (can heal wounds like a Star Trek hand held scanner, etc.).

NanoTech: (Wn90 where 90 is the lowest Workmanship rating % for this tech). This tech is more powerful/expensive/

Cyber Systems Hostilities: BETA

sought after than first gen tech and allows for more interesting abilities (Terminator 2 asshole being able to "melt" and then reform). It allows for more powerful lasers, prisms, smaller robotic spies, androids that appear human, and more "intelligent" AI. The abilities of NanoTech should be akin to the limitations Greater Magic has (able to regrow organs, etc., and then after the tech is done, it must be extracted from the body. In no sense can they be symbionts or biotech).

PicoTech: (Wp99 where 99 is the lowest Workmanship rating % for this tech) EXAMPLE: ColdFusion Battery Wp92 (works 92% of the time because it has been damaged in some way so as to lose some of its Workmanship Rating. This would be the ultimate in tech/most expensive (or priceless), of "Artifact" level enhancements. From this level of tech items will eventually come Celestial Magic (to appear in the Galactic Age) where the Ancient Races learn how to merge their magic with PicoTech to control cold fusion (even hot fission) in very small spaces for grand achievements (open rifts in hyperspace, lasers that can destroy worlds (i.e., the DeathStar), etc.). But for the Cyber Age, they should just be anomalous Artifacts, and there should be few of them. All of this is still external to a living body. An example of PicoTech can be found in the movie Stargate, where the alien Pharaoh had a special metal glove he put on his hand that agitated molecules in his victims whom he killed (remember his guard he killed).

BioTechnologically Enhanced: Nano. BenH-n100 where 100 is the % performance; if biotech is damaged this number degrades. BioTech can be merged and nearly symbiotic with the host (such as it does not need to be removed as does TenH). It is the First Gen tech that can do this and will be relegated to "old news" as soon as the more powerful and more easily hidden BenH-p comes out. Over time, it will be less expensive to obtain, and the masses will be able to purchase it (at first on the black market, and then later in Corporation-approved markets). But they still will be no match for BenH-p Corporate Agents (well, maybe 4 or 5 BenH-n heroes would be able to take down a BenH-p agent). External brain enhancements (for knowledge based skills), external body enhancements that link with the brain on wifi, say (for fists or robotic like perfect manipulation of fingers, arms), etc. [!!] BenH-n must always include external bodily signs: power sources, wires, jacks for recharging, etc. The sole exception to [!!] is when bones or the entire skeleton is replaced with Titanium bone/skeleton. That would still be BenH-n.

BioTechnology Enhanced: Pico. BenH-p100 where 100 is the % performance until degraded by damage. The ultimate, cutting edge, BioTech available. As such, it is guarded against all intrusion and unique to the Corporation that invented it. This is the stuff locked in vaults behind armies of mercs, only to be used upon special command of the Corporate Board.

BenH-p creates super humans capable of astonishment: their skin is actually armor, muscles do not weary and are bonded with the picotech to be stronger, bones like steel (like in BenH-n) but that can change shape at will, extra pico-tech blood pumps (to help the heart provide more oxygen to the body), internal brain enhancements, internal body skill enhancements, etc., characterize this BioTech.

BV = Body Value (can be increased with internal BenH-p)

DV = Defensive Value (can be increased with external armor (or internal BenH-p)

SGY = Synergy. No longer used. UNLESS we should use it to power BenH items.

MTAP = Magical Tapping Power. Only Ancient Races will be able to use this and only for spells that are in the two core rulebooks. Magic cannot be used in conjunction with technology in the Cyber Age.

W:100 = Workmanship with 100% reliability. This is a term that is used for Dead World/Steampunk and might overlap slightly into the beginning of Cyber Age until "perfect" weapons are always reliable. For instance, a poorly made rifle might have a W:20, which means it will only fire successfully (without misfiring, backfiring, or jamming) 20% of the time.

Feel free to come up with other abbreviations and naming conventions you deem necessary as you develop the age. Some might include resistances to Blindness caused by lasers, shock (from electricity), etc.

Must haves

At least five "big-boy" corporations all vying for power

Major personalities (who are the movers and shakers of the Corporations? and which government leaders (Presidents, Kings, Queens, etc.) are their puppets?

Minor personalities (they may not be powerful, but they have major roles to play even if it is that they are red herring nobodies that keep themselves afloat with rumors

Rogue personalities (those who will not kneel to the Corporations) that have their own networks of underground "Freedom"

Geography as it is controlled Corporately. There may well be some free cities/countries still out there that have not yet been economically/corporately conquered... Perhaps even because none of the corporations care enough: the jungles in Africa might have little to offer except for the very rare flower that is needed to cure AIDS; Jerusalem might be a free city because it might not have any natural resources... and so on. Geography alone can create "natural" conflict between nations and corporations...

Cyber Systems Hostilities: BETA

The western hemisphere is open for development geographically (we have to use the maps that are in the Storyteller's book for Europe/Asia/Austrailia). Now it's yours: North and South America. Design them how you wish. Remember, they were probably twisted as well during He Who Stands Alone's Remaking with the SphereTowers.

Technologies separated by era and type (body armor types, weapons, BioTech enhancements, vehicles (how do people get around), etc.). Some BenH-p implants might be able to Download specific skill sets. Costs in CC (CryptoCurrency) and ECC (EliteCryptoCurrency) should be assigned to each item (some items will not be able to be purchased with CC as it is too valuable).

New skills that are applicable to the Cyber Age; New Callings, Vocations

A list of natural disasters that throw chaos into the mix. These disasters are those that man, with all his tech, still has not been able to tame/control. (Meteor showers, volcanoes, earthquakes, etc.). But with a TWIST: some corporations might actually have discovered a TenH-p way to create these natural disasters (remember HAARP technology we have now?).... And just what have all those particle accelerators been able to accomplish? mini black holes?

Who are considered the primitive peoples of the world any more? and why? is it because someone got nuked back to the iron age? and there must be a Corporate reason for leaving them primitive... (Slave selection for the sex trade? After all, androids for sex just might not be an Elite's cup of tea).

Philosophies of each Corporation. What makes the corporations different? How do they attract more people to join them? Do they have codes of honor? What are their goals? I would suggest that the five Corporations are secretly controlled by the five Ancient Races (to add continuity to the "immortal" aspect of the game). So, The Chin Corporation, for example (and perhaps you can think of a much better name than Chin!), would be of an Oshekogan Ancient Race. (The other four ancient races are: Astorian (Roman), Ammorian (black), Atlantean, and Arkadian (natural shapeshifters and a cross between Celts/American indians in culture).

First Page of Character Record

Use the character sheet as the jumping off point. It accurately reflects the feel / flavor I want the game to have. Not all characters will be Ancient Races (in fact, some will be TenH/BenH cyborgs hunting the Ancient Races!!). Only Ancient Race characters have the special VITALS that disperses Head/Torso damage as one body part. All other races (Starborn, Newborn, Androids, etc.) places 35% of the total BV on their torso (simply add LArm, RArm, and one leg to get the 35%), and the rest

of the BV (after 10% for each arm and 15% for each leg) on their head (that is what VITAL2 is; Ancient Races will never use VITAL2).

We've added TAF: Technical Affinity. A person must have a TAF minimum rank of [5] in order to use any BenH-n or BenH-p item (where tech is connected in some manner with the body's biology). That's why 5, 6, 7 are a different color than TAF ranks 1-5. TAF ranks 8,9,10, fall under the "Immortal Ranks" levels and as such yield [B]lue dice to TAF attribute checks.

For Derived Attributes, we've added: BIC (Bionic Capacity), BEN (Bionic Endurance), and ALG (Algorithmic Mastery). Certain Gear Mods, whether they be TenH or BenH, will depend on BIC/BEN/ALG for bonuses and capabilities. If the mod is more brain/intelligence associated, it may well use Algorithmic Mastery. If the mod is more strength-oriented, BIC. If the mod is more repetitive in a physical way, BEN, the idea being that for any mod, the body must interact somehow, and while machines are virtually limitless in endurance/strength, the muscles that attach to, or comply with these mods are not (including brain attention span, for ALG).

On the character sheet, we've included the 2 Gold dice in some of the formulas (like Awareness: [G][G]+TACxd10W + Bonus + [T][F][M][B][P]). We still have the [T]rait, [F]ighting art, [M]agic blue dice from the Adventurer's Rulebook since the player characters will need those, especially if they are role-playing an ancient race immortal that has survived to the Cyber Age. The new [B]ioTech die is also a blue bonus die, and depends on the gear description as to whether they get it.

Tech does not affect MAF or MYS or magic casting at all.

We've made TALENT use (Synergy) for the Cyber Age optional/less important. It will be up to the individual StoryTeller if they want to have Talents in their Cyber Age. But for the official Story, Talents will be a lost art, with the masses gravitating to the much more easily obtainable Cyber mods.

Immortal Power Level Body Value should not be added to the Total BV or Allocated BV. Immortals still get arms, legs cut off. But, their Immortal BV grow them back over several hours (see PHL:Heal Rate). An exception to this is when the Immortal is taking whole body or Magical (whole body) damage. Then the damage is taken off of the Immortal Power Levels first. Also, if an Ancient Race Immortal, the torso cannot be severed from the head; therefore the Immortal BV would kick in. Each Immortal Power Level grants 200BV along with 1 Immortal Gift (see SC43-44). Thus, an immortal could theoretically survive a hydrogen nuke blast of 15000 BV damage simply by being a PL75 Immortal (with Immortal BV = 200 x 75 = 15000); in this example, all of his immortal PLs would be taken away in one phase, but he would still have 200+ BV from his Base and END bonus. As long as an immortal still has 1 BV

Cyber Systems Hostilities: BETA

point in his vitals, he can recover / heal and regenerate his PLs (although it will take months).

OnGrid/OffGrid: this essentially means in the world system or underground/criminal trying to evade the world system. There will be thriving economies for both, especially the latter, where Big Brother has trouble seeing.

The format for advanced weaponry projectiles is AP-nTx where AP is the armor piercing rating, n=number of damage dice to roll, T=Take, and x=the number of dice you get to add from the roll. So, 10-4T3 means that the projectile (a bullet, say) ignores 10 points of armor, and does 3d10 of damage (select 3 highest dice from the 4 rolled). Each projectile/laser/ranged weapon must have a MER (max effective range) that after which it loses the armor piercing rating completely and also 50% of damage per 100Hexes past the MER.

For an in-game example, we'll use a modified sabot round from a tank: MER is 3000 Hexes (meters/yards (for in game we make yards = 1Hx just for ease, even though technically the MER would be 3300 yards)). Let's say the sabot is 200-20T20. That means it would pierce 200 points of armor (about 20 inches of steel armor, easy conversion 10 pts = 1 inch of steel) for 20T20 damage for whatever is under the armor. But past the MER, it would not get ANY armor piercing capability, and at 3100Hexes only do 10T10 damage; at 3200Hexes: 5T5; and after that it's not even worth it.

We'll have to come up with a huge chart for legacy weapons and Cyber Age railgun/laser/microwave/sonic weapons with corresponding AP coefficients and relative accuracy for nTx damage.

Second Page of Character Record.

With some important exceptions, all of the legacy skills from the old character sheet are summed up in an average in the first 5 here: ACADEMIC/SCHolarly, COMBAT/MILitary, etc. The Ancient Race character must add up all ranks of their skills (but not the ones that were culled out and listed separately) and then divide them by the number of skills to get the average and ROUND DOWN (as we always round down in this game). This will be their new legacy skill rank. Those important legacy skills we've listed separately. All legacy skills and Cyber Age common skills have a Cost Modifier (CMod) of 20 (which means it costs 20Fortune Points x the new skill rank to get that skill rank…and they cannot skip ranks).

SPECIALIZATIONs. For any skill not mentioned SPECIFICALLY, the player can opt to have it as a Specialization Skill (even, say, a legacy skill that was on the old character sheet that's not specifically mentioned, like SK:Forgery. This would take Forgery OUT of the Averaged legacy category of ARTISTIC/ART and put it in the specialization section so that it could be

LEARNED BY THE CHARACTER withOUT the need to rely on TenH or BenH technology (up to R5 for White Dice); for ANCIENT RACE characters/immortals from earlier ages, they will most likely do this because the Cost Modifier (20) is lowest and they already have Blue Dice perks from their Traits or Fighting Art Powers or MenH items; still, they will need a BioTech to gain the last Blue Die ([B]). Other more modern and Cyber Age skills (that are not on the legacy character sheet) can also be added in this section as specializations, like "Brain Surgery" or "Rocket/Ballistic Science" or "Laser Weaponry," even by Ancient Races, but they will not have any perks (Blue Dice or other perks) until they spend the Fortune Points (and money) to gain a physical BenH skill mod that allows them to move past "human" limitations on that skill (ability, memory retention, speed of recall, accuracy, speed of performance, perfect technique, etc.). The BenH enhancements move beyond the "human memory" Cost Modifier of 20 and can become quite expensive for the highest-end gear.

The BenH skill mod system.

Each Specialization Skill has 5 important levels of Availability for BIOTECH. (not counting the first level, Common (White) at CMod20, which is just memorization of a skill without TenH/MenH enhancements). They are: Uncommon (Green) at CMod30, Rare (Blue) at CMod40, Pro (Purple) at CMod60, Exotic (Gold) at CMod80, Legendary (Orange Red) at CMod100. Each piece of Tech is one of these five levels. When a player buys/discovers/steals a new piece of tech, they can use it starting at Rank=1. They must buy up the tech with Fortune Points to get better at using that tech, and they must do this for each new Tech that is of a different color. For Example, though a Special Brain Surgery mod is already R4, Player X kills the Zeno Corp's Brain/Tech Surgeon and steals his Legendary Brain Surgery mod. Player X installs the Legendary Mod on himself, but starts with that mod at R1. He must buy the Ranks up for that new mod. If he needs to do brain surgery, he can reinstall the Special Mod he had and gain back his R4 with no problem.

At first this seems shitty, but the reasons for it are:

[1] each Mod comes with its own set of PERKS that must be absorbed: Uncommon Mods= NO PERKS (just the knowledge of that skill); Rare: 1 Perk; Special: 2 Perks, Exotic: 3-4 Perks, Legendary: 5-7 Perks. Perks can be anything from extra [B]lue dice (1 per perk), to special abilities like "At will adhesiveness" (for a spiderman suit). Maybe a PERK can be a Rank, so a Legendary Gear might have a R5 Brain Surgery, with 2 more perks available for the max 7. Note that while the character must start over as far as WHITE dice rank (they always get R1 free for any BenH Mod), they receive all the Perks as soon as the BenH gear is "plugged" in to their body peripherals.

Cyber Systems Hostilities: BETA

[2] With each mod level (common/uncommon/rare/pro/exotic/legendary) the Sphere of Knowledge grows exponentially. See examples.

EXAMPLE 1: An uncommon mod for Chemistry at R5 would know everything there is to know about Chemistry in order to teach High School. Rare R5: teach college. Special R5: Make any illicit drug or dangerous substance (acid). Exotic R5: research/make cures for all diseases and poisons. Legendary R5 do all of that for dozens of different environments/planets/vacuum/gravity/ etc. Burden for this type of breakdown will rest with the Storyteller, but we will have examples of several popular mods along this line of thinking.

EXAMPLE 2: Hacking Mod: Common (no mod): hack computers, Uncommon: hack surveillance and security systems; Rare: hack communications systems (phone/cell towers/internet and some hardware (auto-driving cars/gps/unmanned flight systems); Special (hack power grids/satellites/low-level corporate networks/android MK1 systems); exotic (hack BioTech systems/android MK2 systems/mid-level corporate networks/low-funded or older mercenary military systems); legendary (hack high level corporate networks/secure military installations and bots/LEO comms/Anything Darknet).

EXAMPLE 3: Bionic Legs: Common (no mod) Run 4x MVT rate. Uncommon:Run up to 30mph for ten hours straight, can jump 3 stories up or fall 3 stories without taking any damage; Rare: Run up to 50mph for 20 hours straight, can jump 5 stories up or fall 5 stories without taking any damage; Special: can kick through thick brick and mortar without damage, jump/fall 10 stories, run 100mph; Exotic: same as special but can kick through steel, lift two tons with knee joint as long as upper half of leg is leveraged; Legendary: can do all that but also legs move so fast as to be able to run across water, or point the feet down in order to penetrate 10 feet of cement if falling down from at least a 10 story height. The R0 to R5 is just how good you are able to do what you can do at the uncommon - legendary level.

A Legendary Mod is almost NEVER for sale, as they are so unique as to be heavily guarded or actually used by the multiple badasses in the game.

NOTES:

On the following pages, we've placed the Cyber Age BETA Character Records (they might get tweaked a little or include different stats we find we need). Your feedback is always welcome as well!

Immortal Empires™
Cyber Age Character Record

ORank

NAME | EXPERIENCE | FORTUNE POINTS | RACE | AGE | SEX | EYES/HAIR | WEIGHT | GLORY | FP RATIO

1 2 3 4 5 6 7 8 9 10   1 2 3 4 5 6 7 8 9 10
1 2 3 4 5 6 7 8 9 10   1 2 3 4 5 6 7 8 9 10
1 2 3 4 5 6 7 8 9 10   1 2 3 4 5 6 7 8 9 10

MAIN ATTRIBUTES | Immortal MAX | Common Abilities | BioTech Modifiers | DERIVED ATTRIBUTES

Attribute	Scale		Common Abilities			BioTech	
PHQ	1 2 3 4 5 6 7	8 9 10	DAMAGE +	FEAT OF STR	MAX WEIGHT	+/- RANK	NET PHQ
PHL	1 2 3 4 5 6 7	8 9 10	HEAL RATE	ATTRACTION	NATURAL DV	+/- RANK	NET PHL
AGL	1 2 3 4 5 6 7	8 9 10	REACT BONUS	REFLEXES	NATRL JUMP	+/- RANK	NET AGL
COR	1 2 3 4 5 6 7	8 9 10	ATTACK BONUS	BALANCE	SIDE BY SIDE	+/- RANK	NET COR
INT	1 2 3 4 5 6 7	8 9 10	MEMORIZED	ACCURACY	TRUE SPELLS	+/- RANK	NET INT
INS	1 2 3 4 5 6 7	8 9 10	TRIAL SPELL +	CONTROLD MR	ENCRYPT	+/- RANK	NET INS
WIL	1 2 3 4 5 6 7	8 9 10	COGNITIVE CH	CLOSED MIND	PRESIST +	+/- RANK	NET WIL
EMP	1 2 3 4 5 6 7	8 9 10	FEEL EMOTION	GROUPTHINK	SIXTH SENSE	+/- RANK	NET EMP
MAF	1 2 3 4 5 6 7	8 9 10	SENSE CAST	MTAP RECOVER	ACTIVE SPELLS	X-Pts	UFP
TAF	1 2 3 4 5 6 7	8 9 10	ACTV BIOTECH	REMOTE RNGE	JAMMER RES		

DERIVED ATTRIBUTES

TAC TECHNICAL ACUITY	1 2 3 4 5 6 =	[INS] + [INT] + [EMP]	/5
SOC SOCIAL PROWESS	1 2 3 4 5 6 =	[EMP] + [PHQ] + [WIL]	/5
CBT COMBAT ABILITY	1 2 3 4 5 6 =	[AGL] + [COR] + [PHQ]	/5
END BODILY ENDURANCE	1 2 3 4 5 6 =	[MAF] + [PHL] + [WIL]	/5
ART ARTISTIC APTITUDE	1 2 3 4 5 6 =	[AGL] + [COR] + [INS]	/5
MYS MYSTICAL TALENT	1 2 3 4 5 6 =	[INT] + [MAF] + [PHL]	/5
BIC BIONIC CAPACITY	1 2 3 4 5 6 =	[PHQ] + [AGL] + [TAF]	/5
BEN BIONIC ENDURANCE	1 2 3 4 5 6 =	[WIL] + [PHL] + [TAF]	/5
ALG ALGORITHMIC MASTERY	1 2 3 4 5 6 =	[INS] + [INT] + [TAF]	/5

BODY VALUE (BV) | BIOTECH BV | DEFENSIVE VALUE (DV)

TOTAL BV	=	BASE BV	+	END X 20	+	BONUS	+		TOTAL BODY MDV	TOTAL BODYSUIT DV

IMMORTAL POWER LEVELS (200BV EACH)

	ALLOCATED BV	CURRENT BV	DV by PART		NATURAL DV	ARMOR DV	BIOTECH DV
L. ARM 10%				=		+	+
R. ARM 10%				=		+	+
L. LEG 15%				=		+	+
R. LEG 15%				=		+	+
VITALS THE REST / 35%				=		+	+
VITAL2 HEAD (THE REST)				=		+	+

AWARENESS
[ ] [ ] + TAC d10W+ BONUS + T F M B P

MAGIC RESISTANCE
[ ] [ ] + MYS d10W+ BONUS + T F M B P

PHYSICAL RESISTANCE
[ ] [ ] + CBT d10W+ BONUS + T F M B P

VITALS PRESIST CHECKS
	75%	50%	25%
VITALS BV AT:			
PRESIST TN:	20	30	40
PENALTY IF FAIL:	P	P P	OUT

TN		2TN
10	EASY PEASY	1
20	EASY	2
30	MODERATE	3
40	DIFFICULT	4
50	VERY HARD	5
75	IMPOSSIBLE	7
100	TECH CRIT	10

MAGICAL TAPPING POWER (MTAP)

CORRUPTED

TOTAL = MAF x 50 + MYS X 100 + VARIABLE + BONUS - FA COST

CURRENT MTAP

ENCHANTMENT BOUND 1	ENCHANTMENT BOUND 2	ENCHANTMENT BOUND 3	ENCHANTMENT BOUND 4
ITEM / RETURN RANGE	ITEM / RETURN RANGE	ITEM / RETURN RANGE	ITEM / RETURN RANGE

ACTIVE SPELLS

SPELL	BINDING	SPELL	BINDING

MAGICAL CONTROL (MCTRL)

SIZE OF SPELL	CAST TN	MCTRL		
TO	15	MINOR =	STANDARD	/2
TO	25	STANDARD =	MYS x 20 + MAGIC RK + PHL x 2 + BONUS	
TO	40	MAJOR =	MINOR + STANDARD	
PUSH	50			

ANCHORED SPELLS

MYS	SPELL NAME	POTENCY	TRIGGER: UP TO 5 WORDS
1			
2			
3			
4			
5			

PHASE COMBAT

WEAPON	PhACT	PRIMARY ATTACK ROLL	DAMAGE
	[ ] [ ] + RANK d10W+ CBT + T F M B P		
	[ ] [ ] + RANK d10W+ CBT + T F M B P		
	[ ] [ ] + RANK d10W+ CBT + T F M B P		
	[ ] [ ] + RANK d10W+ CBT + T F M B P		

MOVEMENT = CBT + TECH + BONUS + MAGIC + 3

REACTION [ ] [ ] + CBT d10W+ BONUS + T F M B P

SYNERGY
MAX	Sum of Main Attr + Ranks x5	BONUS
RECOVER	Sum of Derived Attribute Ranks x2	

SOCIAL STATUS

JOB TITLE	ON GRID	OFF GRID	PROFESSION
SOCIAL WORTH		OR	STREET CRED
SUCCESS REP			SUCCESS REP
NETWORK	P		ILL NETWORK
	P		
	P		
ON GRID			OFF GRID

+ [ ] [ ] +

Immortal Empires™
Cyber Age Character Record

CHARACTER MOTTO

LEGACY SKILLS CMod /20

| TAC | | CBT | | ART | | BIC | | ALG | |
| SOC | | END | | MYS | | BEN | | AND | |

Skill	Levels	Options
ACADEMIC/SCH	1 2 3 4 5	T F M B P
COMBAT/MIL	1 2 3 4 5	T F M B P
ARTISTIC/ART	1 2 3 4 5	T F M B P
OUTDOOR/ATH	1 2 3 4 5	T F M B P
SOCIAL/POL	1 2 3 4 5	T F M B P
ACUMEN	1 2 3 4 5	T F M B P

Skill	Levels	Options
CASTING MAGIC	1 2 3 4 5	T F M P P
COMBAT DODGE	1 2 3 4 5	T F M B P
LYING	1 2 3 4 5	T F M B P
SEDUCTION	1 2 3 4 5	T F M B P
STEALTH	1 2 3 4 5	T F M B P
SURPRISE	1 2 3 4 5	T F M B P

CYBER AGE COMMON SKILLS

ON GRID

Skill	Levels	Options
CORPORATE LAW	1 2 3 4 5	T F M B P
HOME SECURITY	1 2 3 4 5	T F M B P
KISSING ASS	1 2 3 4 5	T F M B P
NEGOTIATION	1 2 3 4 5	T F M B P
SNITCH TACTICS	1 2 3 4 5	T F M B P
SOCIAL MEDIA	1 2 3 4 5	T F M B P

OFF GRID

Skill	Levels	Options
EVASION	1 2 3 4 5	T F M B P
HACKING	1 2 3 4 5	T F M B P
HOT DRIVING	1 2 3 4 5	T F M B P
INTIMIDATION	1 2 3 4 5	T F M B P
STREET SAVVY	1 2 3 4 5	T F M B P
SURVEILLANCE	1 2 3 4 5	T F M B P

SPECIALIZATION

CMod /30 CMod /40 CMod /60 CMod /80 CMod /100

BenH SKILL MODS

ITEMS EQUIPPED

POWER BASES

SOCIO-ECONOMIC	
CORPORATE	
PARA-MILITARY	
OFF-GRID	
INFILTRATED	
MAGICAL